"Stacy Hawkins Adams weaves a . . . stirring tale of grace and adversity [that] will keep readers turning pages long into the night. *Nothing but the Right Thing* is just that. Don't miss it."

Marilynn Griffith, author, *Made of Honor* and *Pink*

"*Nothing but the Right Thing* is an outstanding heartfelt and compelling novel about faith, love, friendship, and forgiveness."

Kimberley Brooks, author, *He's Fine . . . But Is He Saved?*

"After the last page you'll walk away with another dose of faith, a new hope for your dreams, and a realization that walking with God is nothing but the right thing!"

Tia McCollors, author, *A Heart of Devotion* and *Zora's Cry*

"Adams's *Nothing but the Right Thing* is surely that . . . the right thing for women struggling with long-suffering, maternity, family responsibility, and faith—not only to read but to study and to comfort their souls. Illuminating with great integrity."

Dee Stewart, Christian Fiction News

"Adams writes with a human touch and delightful storytelling ability and conveys a powerful message of life and love. I was captivated and deeply moved from the first to the last page."

Marina Woods, founder and editor in chief,
www.goodgirlbookclubonline.com

Nothing but the Right Thing

Nothing but the Right Thing

a novel

Stacy Hawkins Adams

Revell

Grand Rapids, Michigan

© 2006 by Stacy Hawkins Adams

Published by Fleming H. Revell
a division of Baker Publishing Group
P.O. Box 6287, Grand Rapids, MI 49516-6287
www.revellbooks.com

Printed in the United States of America

Library of Congress Cataloging-in-Publication Data
Adams, Stacy Hawkins, 1971–
    Nothing but the right thing : a novel / Stacy Hawkins Adams.
        p.   cm.
    ISBN 10: 0-8007-3097-6 (pbk.)
    ISBN 978-0-8007-3097-0 (pbk.)
    1. Miscarriage—Fiction. 2. Abused women—Fiction. 3. Teenagers—
Fiction. I. Title.
PS3601.D396N68 2006
813'.6—dc22   2005033659

To Joy, for your courage,
and to Barbara Rascoe,
for your friendship and support

In memory of my beloved mother,
Dorothy Ann Hawkins

My soul, wait silently for God alone,
For my expectation is from Him.

Psalm 62:5

1

The first blow split her lip, then his fist kissed her eye. By the third time her beloved slammed his shiny knuckles into her soft flesh, Erika Tyler Wilson had decided.

This was it. Tonight's one-sided boxing match would be her last.

Elliott would hold her tight, as usual, and try to kiss away the pain of the bruises he had inflicted. He would cradle her in his embrace and wipe her tears, whispering in her ear how much he loved her. Tomorrow, though, the dozen yellow roses he always sent after a particularly brutal episode would be coming to an empty house.

As she lay there in a child-sized, crumpled heap, covering her face and head with her arms, she told herself this would be the last time she would cower on the floor of this house. No more worries about removing bloodstains from the snow white carpet. No more wondering if the neighbors were peering through their palladium windows to get their weekly entertainment—same time, same place, same guest star.

No more excuses. No more shame. No more pain. Erika felt free, even as Elliott continued lashing out at her.

"Why—do—you—make—me—do—this—to—you—?"

He punctuated each word with a blow as he called her a foul name—again.

She knew the routine. When he began spouting ugly words, it meant the end of his tirade was near. Erika locked herself into a corner of her mind, away from the pain. She felt her husband hitting her, but then again she didn't.

In this space she was safe. She didn't think about anything, really, except getting through the beating. By removing herself from the present, she could keep her sanity.

She often lifted her thoughts above what her body was enduring so that when Elliott was ready to make up, she could comply without hating herself. If she forced her mind to disengage from the abuse, she couldn't remember everything that happened.

The process made it easier to look into her husband's clear brown eyes and believe him when he said he was sorry. It made it easier to believe what she always told herself: he couldn't help it. He really hadn't meant to hurt her, but once again she had done something foolish to provoke him.

Erika always managed to upset Elliott, with her probing questions, with her inadequate efforts to be the dutiful wife of a law firm partner, or simply with her failure to have dinner on the table when he arrived home from a stressful day at work.

"Don't I work hard enough so you can stay home? The least you can do is have a hot meal ready for me. Is that too much to ask?" Elliott would sneer as he sat in the cavernous dining room, loosening his tie and waiting to be served like a king.

His after-work routine never veered too much off course. He rarely entered the house the same way, always coming in quietly, as if to catch Erika in an illegal act. Sometimes he would casually enter through the garage door off the kitchen, sometimes through the front door, and other times through the entrance off the side patio. On occasion he would use the entrance to the walk-out basement and startle Erika by emerging in the foyer as she stood in front of the stove putting the finishing touches on their meal.

Elliott would stroll past her without speaking, pick up the dry martini she had waiting for him, and stand with his feet spread apart in front of the bay window that took up most of the rear wall of the kitchen. He would gaze at the golf course, though he couldn't see much because it was usually late evening and too dark.

Instead of relaxing him, the routine seemed to fuel his frustration. It seemed to be his quiet time to dream up a grievance that would give him an excuse good enough to pick a fight. If it wasn't about dinner, the problem would be an errand Erika had forgotten to run or the inappropriate tone she had used when she finally summoned the courage to welcome him home for the evening.

The reason never mattered. When his mood soured, when he felt like swinging, she would enter the ring whether she had asked for the match or not. It had been that way since they had eloped in Jamaica four years earlier. Even in that idyllic retreat, Elliott hadn't been able to control himself.

"Why do you make me hurt you?"

It seemed he had been asking that question in a pained, remorseful whine for as long as she could remember, even before she had become his wife. Funny how she thought their vows would make things better. Not funny how much worse life had become.

Now he was finished. He had grown tired quickly tonight. *The trial today must have been particularly grueling*, Erika thought as she let her mind return to the present.

Elliott knelt beside her and picked her up. In his muscular arms, she felt as light as a paperweight. She struggled to recall a time when she had felt safe there too.

She kept her eyes closed as he carried her up to their bedroom. A single tear slid down the side of her cheek as she rested her head on Elliott's chest.

"I love you, baby," her tall, honey-complexioned husband said softly as he lay her on their king-size bed.

Any other night she would have concentrated on keeping her bloody lips off the sand-and-gold comforter, but tonight she didn't care. She shook with silent sobs as Elliott peppered her with kisses. He didn't seem to notice.

"Why do you make me act this way?" he asked as he closed his eyes and kissed her neck. "Why do you always make me hurt you? I love you.

"Stop crying, baby. I still love you," Elliott whispered into Erika's hair. "Let me show you how much."

Erika stopped shaking as Elliott began to peel off her clothes. Her tears dried up as she lay there and stared at the ceiling. Tonight she was grateful he hadn't bothered to look into her eyes.

If he had, he would have known she was leaving. He

might have tried to kill her. Instead, he apologized and expressed his affection in the best way he knew how.

As usual, he didn't notice Erika's lackluster response to his fervent lovemaking. He mistook her stillness for enjoyment. And when he was done, he lay next to her and told her again that he loved her.

He pulled her close to him and gently kissed her swollen lips.

"Good night, baby. Happy anniversary."

2

Sweat slithered down Serena's back as she reached into the trunk to fish out the last box of knickknacks.

"If it gets any hotter in Richmond this summer, I might as well move to Florida," she muttered under her breath as she repositioned the weight of the load in her arms and turned toward the house. Before she took a step, Micah was at her side.

"Give me that."

He gave Serena a light peck on the lips as he took the large brown box. She smiled gratefully and followed him up the incline and into the garage. She had parked on the street in front of their new house because the movers had taken over the driveway to unload their furniture.

"Remind me again why we bought a house on a hill?" she asked Micah as she trudged up the driveway. "Were we thinking this steep pavement could serve as our Stairmaster?"

She wiped sweat from her neck with the palm of her hand and rubbed the wetness on her grubby strawberry red shorts.

"Well, now, the Bible talks about the importance of a firm foundation," Micah teased.

He smiled, his white teeth glistening in contrast to his smooth ebony skin. Even in normal conversation, the richness of his baritone made him sound as if he were doing the voice-over for a commercial.

Micah put the box on top of several others stacked next to the garage wall and leaned against them. He motioned for Serena to come to him. She smiled back as she complied.

"There you go with that silly look on your face," she said. "Are you about to get all sentimental again?"

Micah pulled her toward him and rested his chin on her shoulder. He leaned into the nape of her neck and smelled her familiar scent.

"What if I am? Welcome home, love."

Serena squeezed him tightly and kissed the tip of his nose. That gesture had been one of her unspoken gifts to him since they wed three years ago.

She pulled away and looked into Micah's eyes. The look he gave her in return let her know he understood: she wished her mother were here to see her dream home, to take a tour, and to ooh and aah over everything.

Even before Serena became Mrs. McDaniels, Micah had been there for her, sticking close as she grieved after Mama's death. He had let her dampen countless shirts.

Sometimes there were no words for the sorrow she felt. He would hold her hand in those moments, and she would rest her head on his chest. When she didn't have the words to ask God for comfort, Micah spoke them for her.

The one thing that had given her peace was the fact

that she and Mama had reconnected before her death. Mama had finally shared her reasons for not telling the truth about Serena's biological father, something Serena had stayed angry about for too long.

She and Mama had forgiven each other, but Serena had still been crushed by her death. Four years later she still craved Mama's voice when she needed advice, understanding without having to explain herself, or a safe place to leave her worries. Mama had been her haven from the world, even when she hadn't accepted the love.

Then Serena had lost Erika. When Erika eloped with Elliott, a sea swelled between the two longtime friends despite the fact that they lived minutes apart.

After Mama's funeral Elliott had refused to allow his new bride to spend much time with Serena. He monitored Erika's every move and decided whose phone calls she could take.

The friendship died, for all intents and purposes, after Erika agreed to serve as Serena's matron of honor, with Elliott's blessing, but didn't show up for the ceremony. To this day Erika hadn't explained why she had come to the rehearsal the night before but was a no-show for the wedding.

Serena had lost a sister. But she knew that until Erika chose to remove herself from Elliott's grip, their friendship couldn't survive.

As Serena stood in front of Micah this morning, gazing into his eyes, her own welled up with tears at her memories. She longed for Erika almost as much as she longed for Mama. Her husband's eyes softened, and she realized that even though he didn't know what to do with her display of emotion, he cared.

Just as Micah had helped her, Serena had been there for him when he had finished seminary with questions about what God wanted him to do. Was he supposed to lead a church, work in youth ministry, or do something totally different?

He had taken a night job at the Brook Road headquarters of the Richmond Post Office as he prayed his way through what Serena began to call his holding pattern. As he circled around the same questions and continued to pray, she had reassured him that God would eventually answer.

"He'll speak to you in his own time," she had told Micah, repeating words he had once used to see her through valleys.

When he had been hired as the full-time pastor of a growing, well-respected church in South Richmond, not far from one of the city's toughest neighborhoods, Serena had been thrilled.

Soon after, he took her to the restaurant on Brown's Island where they had first met, and amid the noonday rush, he got down on his knee and proposed. They wed six months later, with Serena's favorite cousin, Imani, standing nearby as the teary-eyed, six-months-pregnant matron of honor.

Now here Serena and Micah were, moving into their second home, a brick-front, Georgian-style house that was three times the size of their previous residence. Serena's years as a successful advertising executive had been lucrative. Between her savings and Micah's, they had been able to afford a house they had considered well out of their reach and, in some ways, their comfort zone.

Both of them loved the three-bedroom colonial they had purchased in Richmond's Ginter Park neighborhood soon after marrying. It had been perfect for their needs then.

They used one spare bedroom as an office and the other as a guest room, mostly for Micah's mother, who visited from Oklahoma every six months.

But the desire for more space for the growing family they were anticipating had led them to begin looking. Cobblestone Creek, one of Chesterfield County's most highly regarded neighborhoods, was now their new home. Serena couldn't believe she had left her cherished North Side to become a suburbanite.

Before she could chide Micah again for making her a traitor, tinkling laughter drew Serena's attention to the sidewalk in front of their home. A woman trotted by, pushing a double stroller that bore a chubby-cheeked toddler and a sleeping infant, both of whom had the same shade of shocking red hair as hers.

The woman smiled and waved at Serena and Micah but didn't interrupt. Serena and Micah returned the gestures.

"That will be us soon, love," Micah said softly.

Serena's eyes trailed the woman and her children as they turned the corner. She nodded.

After two miscarriages, Serena's spirit was tender. She had lost one baby six weeks into the pregnancy and the other at eleven weeks, just as they were preparing to share the news with everyone.

Micah had come home three months ago, just weeks

after she had miscarried the second time, and announced that he wanted to move.

"If we're going to start a family, we need more space," he had said.

She had fallen into his arms that night and cried for her lost babies but also because Micah's wanting to move gave her hope that eventually they would cradle a child of their own.

When their colonial sold in ten days, she and Micah had both shed tears. Serena had never seen him cry over the lost babies; she knew he was finally releasing the pain.

Today was a milestone. Serena unlocked herself from Micah's embrace and pulled him away from the boxes.

"Let's go inside. Our new neighbors are probably staring, like the woman who just waved."

"Let 'em look," Micah said with a mock attitude as he followed her from the garage into the oblong, sunlit kitchen. "We're married folks."

The two stood side by side in the middle of the room, taking in the first floor of their new home. A team of professional movers bustled nearby, placing furniture in the positions Serena had marked with masking tape.

Neither she nor Micah spoke. She suspected he was giving thanks again, just as she was.

When Serena was a top-notch advertising executive, she and Micah could have easily afforded this home. But when they decided to start their family, Serena had taken a significant pay cut to switch to a less stressful job.

For the most part, her work as executive director of the nonprofit Children's Art Coalition allowed her to work eight hours a day, five days a week. There were monthly board meetings and occasional after-hours functions, but the schedule was much less demanding.

With Micah's salary as a pastor and Serena's more modest income, Cobblestone Creek still had been in their price range. The house they now stood in, though, was in the priciest section of the subdivision.

Serena and Micah had been looking for something smaller when their realtor, Ruby Nelson, called and declared that she had found the perfect property.

"Rev. McDaniels, the owners are moving to Australia in three weeks. An executive recruiting firm has secured the husband a fabulous job. His new company offered to sell the house for him, but he's eager to have everything resolved before he leaves, so he and his wife are selling it for a steal," Ruby had said before catching herself. "Sorry, Reverend, I didn't really mean *steal*."

Micah laughed.

"Please, Ruby. Preachers like bargains too."

The five-bedroom, five-thousand-square-foot house was on the market for about sixty thousand dollars less than its value.

"What's wrong with it?" Micah asked. "Better yet, what's wrong with the owners?"

A thorough check by a certified house inspector turned up few flaws.

On the day Micah and Serena closed, their real estate attorney gave them a letter from the previous owners, to be opened once they had signed the documents to make the house legally theirs.

"My wife and I were young once, just starting out with hope, love, and faith," the executive wrote. "Twenty years of marriage and four children later, our needs have been met many times over. We don't know you personally, but we wish you the best. Enjoy the house as much as we did."

So here they stood, on a Monday morning, marveling and thanking God.

"I don't know what he's getting ready to do with us here, but I'm in the game," Serena said as she put her arms around Micah's waist.

He rubbed her neck.

"Let's play, love."

3

Erika's heart pounded as if she were competing in a NASCAR race and Elliott was driving the car grazing her bumper.

Was she really doing this? Could she leave everything behind and start over on her own? What would people say?

She settled into her seat on the train and took several deep breaths, slowly exhaling each time. She closed her eyes and pushed away the doubt. When she had calmed herself, she finally looked out of the window at the blur of small towns Amtrak was whizzing through.

Yes, I am doing this, she answered herself. *Yes, I can leave the mini mansion, the furs, the cars, the prestige, and most importantly, the abuse.*

And for the first time in her thirty-two years, for the first time since she had begun dating Elliott in college thirteen years earlier, Erika decided she would not worry about what people would say.

As those thoughts liberated her, others threatened to strangle her. Her doubts mushroomed.

Was she absolutely sure she had done the right thing by leaving her husband? He was the kind of man other women longed to call their own: handsome, charming, and successful. What more could a woman want?

What if he comes after me? What if I decide I want to go home?

She knew if she ever did that, Elliott would make her life unbearable. He might even hire a nanny to watch her while he worked.

She chuckled at the notion.

"He's sick enough to do something like that too," she muttered.

Then the tears came.

Erika doubled over with sobs and held herself as she thought about all that her life with Elliott had been and all that it should have been. She covered her mouth with the palm of her hand to stifle the scream that wanted to rip free.

The glistening diamond on her ring finger caught her eye. Erika twisted off the two-carat ring and held it before her eyes. It was beautiful. It shone, as always, because Elliott insisted she have it cleaned by the jewelers every other month.

When she looked good, from her hair, which he had insisted she grow past her shoulders, to her ring finger to her shoes, then he looked good, he had often reminded her.

Erika slid the ring into the small black purse on the seat next to her and wiped her cheeks with the back of her hand.

"Today is a new beginning," she whispered over and over.

That's what the hotline operator had told her just after midnight, when she had slipped away from the sleeping Elliott and driven the Land Rover to the WaWa gas station ten miles from their home, on Route 10.

This wasn't the first time Erika had called the Family Violence Hotline, but the volunteer on the other end of the phone tonight seemed to realize that Erika was serious about leaving.

"What is your zip code? What belongings do you have with you?" the woman asked.

Although Elliott had been in a deep sleep when Erika had gotten out of the bed with excruciating slowness, she had tiptoed to the closet and slid into a pair of jeans and a partially faded sea green T-shirt.

She had stayed just long enough to collect her jacket and the three hundred dollars she had been stashing from the grocery money for the past four months. Elliott kept close tabs on their income, as he did every other aspect of their relationship.

Surprisingly, though, he hadn't seemed to miss twenty dollars here and there. As the beatings had intensified, she had begun creating a stash as a security blanket of sorts.

Erika had slid her feet into her sneakers and put on a tan baseball cap. She had inched past the bed and out the door.

Elliott hadn't stirred. For once she was thankful that instead of going to sleep after kissing her goodnight he had decided to cap the night off with another drink. This time it was champagne, in honor of their anniversary. He had insisted that she have a glass too, but in his self-absorption, he hadn't noticed that she took two sips to his three glasses. Before she knew it, he had dozed off.

Erika hadn't exhaled until she had turned out of the circular driveway and traveled three blocks with no sign of Elliott tailing her.

The hotline volunteer advised her to abandon the black SUV at the gas station with the key locked inside. She told Erika to use some of her cash to call a taxi.

"It's safer for you to leave it there. Otherwise, your husband will report the vehicle missing and have police looking for you. You won't be in trouble, but the authorities will have helped your husband get you home."

The woman paused.

"You sure you're ready?"

Erika was honest.

"I'm not sure of anything right now," she said, her voice quivering. "Except that I can't take him hitting me anymore."

The woman asked if Erika had family who would be looking for her.

"Well, let's see," Erika said, unable to squelch the resentment that surfaced whenever she thought about her mother. "Dear old Mom ran off to Minnesota with a man she met on the Internet two years ago, and I haven't seen her since. She sends postcards or emails every so often just to let me know she's having the time of her life. I haven't found the time to let her know that I am too."

The volunteer moved to the next question.

"Do you have any close friends or co-workers your husband will harass if he's trying to find you?"

The fact that she had no one in her life who cared that

much about her right now made Erika ill. Elliott had helped alienate her from her real estate colleagues and anyone else who tried to get to know her.

Two months into their marriage, he had insisted that she quit working. He didn't want his wife driving people all over Richmond to show houses for sale when she should be home tending to her own, he had said.

As she gripped the pay phone, her thoughts turned to Serena. She blinked to fight back tears and answered the woman's question.

"No close friends."

The volunteer didn't seemed surprised.

"The good thing, then, is that your husband will have less ability to track you down. If you're not trying to keep in touch with friends or family he'll know to harass about you, it's easier to make a clean break."

Within minutes the volunteer booked Erika on a train to Washington, D.C.

"When you get there, you'll be met at Union Station by a woman named Charlotte. She'll take you to Naomi's Nest, where you can stay as long as you need if they see that you're making efforts to become independent.

"If you change your mind and decide to go back to your husband, meet him at Union Station or some other neutral spot," the woman said firmly. "Do not, under any circumstances, tell him where the shelter is located. The other women living there must not be put in jeopardy."

By the time Erika arrived at the train station on Staples Mill Road, it was four o'clock in the morning. She felt like a mouse dodging a trap.

As she had sat in the station, waiting to board under

the name Hope Waters, Erika had kept her head lowered, making only her eyes visible below the baseball cap. She had scanned the seating area every few minutes. With only five other people in the lobby, it had been easy to keep track of who was coming and going.

She had been grateful when she got on the train and saw that no one was seated nearby. She could cry in peace.

Now she wiped a fresh flood of tears from her cheeks and continued gazing out the window at nothing in particular.

She thought about the hotline volunteer's questions regarding people close to her.

Nobody cares if I live or die, she told herself. *Do I even care?*

Serena came to mind again. For the first time since their estrangement, Erika allowed herself to think about how much she missed her friend.

Even after all this time, somehow she knew Serena would never forsake her.

4

I do not need this ice cream," Serena said as she pulled the carton from the freezer. "Just a little . . ."

By the time she had put the third scoop of marble chocolate fudge in her bowl, Micah had strolled in with the mail.

"Fix me some too?" he asked without looking up.

Serena laughed.

"What about the diet we're supposed to be on? Fifteen pounds each, remember?"

"I see you have three scoops. Give me four."

Micah continued rifling through the stack of mail.

"Here's a letter from Turner One," he said. "When was the last time you talked to Max?"

Serena was still good friends with her former boss at the advertising agency where she had been employed for six years. When she had informed him that she wanted to find a job with a less hectic pace so she and Micah could start a family, Max had been very supportive.

"I'll hate losing you, Serena. You're part of the family,"

he had said. "But I understand when different seasons in life beckon. I'll do whatever I can to help you."

A glowing recommendation from Max had helped her land the executive director position at the Children's Art Coalition eighteen months ago. She loved the job.

"I had lunch with Max two weeks ago; he didn't tell me to expect anything," Serena told Micah.

She slid the envelope from his hand and scooped a spoonful of ice cream into her mouth. She could have passed for a college model in her jeans and sleeveless tangerine silk blouse, with her silky black hair caught up in a neat bun and her flawless cinnamon skin aglow. Micah told her that often. Forget the fifteen pounds she thought she needed to lose.

"It's in all the right places," he'd tell her when she complained.

"Yours too," she would tease and pat his getting-plump belly. He still looked like Denzel's younger cousin, though.

She opened the envelope from Max and read slowly to decipher his handwriting.

Serena, it was great to see you recently. Thanks for treating your old boss to lunch. Makes me proud to see you doing so well.

I'm leaving the country on business tonight; otherwise, I would call and share this information. Vickie received two phone calls for you at the office earlier this week and thought they were odd enough to share with me.

An Elliott Wilson called first, demanding that he be given your new work information. He sounded

29

agitated, so Vickie declined to tell him and rushed him off the phone.

Serena frowned and looked up from Max's letter.

"Elliott tried to call me at Turner One," she told Micah as she kept reading.

About a week later, Vickie got a call from your friend Erika. Vickie remembered that you two had been close but thought it was odd that Erika no longer knew how to reach you. She said she felt comfortable telling Erika you had moved on, but as a precaution, she only gave Erika your email address.

Serena laid the letter on the granite island in the center of the kitchen.

"Something strange is going on. Erika called me too."

Micah, who was sitting at the small table in the breakfast nook, looked up from what was left of his ice cream.

"You think she finally left him?"

Serena abandoned her bowl and answered him as she turned to run upstairs to find her laptop.

"I don't know what's going on, but Vickie gave her my email address at the coalition. I'm going to check it now."

Micah was right behind her.

It took just a few seconds to log on to the coalition's computer system. Serena often did so from home when she wanted to work after hours. She hadn't checked her email all week, though, because she had taken time off to concentrate on the move.

The email prompt showed she had twenty-five new messages.

The first one had been sent at 9:03 p.m. four days ago. It was from someone called Shadow. The sender had used a free Internet account.

Serena opened the email and read it quickly.

Serena, now would be the perfect time for the four-word cliché: I told you so. You could whisper, yell, or spit those words at me right now, and all I would do is hang my head in shame. I deserve to hear those words, because as I'm writing to you, I'm sitting in a shelter for battered women. I can't tell you where I am, for safety reasons—yours and mine—but I can tell you that I've never forgotten how truthful you were with me.

You told me not to marry him. You told me if he hit me, he really didn't love me. You said it all in love, but I didn't want to hear you. Now your long-ago warnings keep swirling through my brain. If only I had listened.

I guess dwelling on the past doesn't help much now. But I wanted to say I'm sorry for being too stupid to hear you. And I've never apologized for standing you up at your wedding. I am so sorry.

I remember how you used to talk about God being real and how there is power in prayer. I used to roll my eyes and crack jokes. Maybe I'm beginning to believe you now. If it weren't for some kind of higher power, I don't know how I could have walked away from Elliott.

If he calls and says he's searching for me, please don't tell him about this email. I wanted to write and let you know that I'm finally free from his grip. Even though I've abused our friendship, I hope you can forgive me. And I'd appreciate your prayers. Knowing your belief in God, I'm sure that no matter where I am, or where you are, they can touch me. Love, E.

Erika had signed the email with the nickname Serena had given her when they were in college. Serena closed the email but continued to stare at the screen.

Erika had finally left Elliott? After all of these years? Miracles did happen. But her friend sounded like she was in so much pain. Serena knew her chances of locating Erika in a shelter were slim, but she had to try.

"We have to find her," she said softly to Micah, who had been standing behind her, reading over her shoulder. "I have to be there for her."

5

Micah closed the door to the room he had chosen as his study. He quickly navigated the brown boxes scattered across the floor to reach the cherry rolltop desk that had once belonged to his grandfather. The movers had positioned it against the far wall, just below a small octagon window.

He rolled the leather chair out and sat at the desk for the first time since the move.

"Welcome to Cobblestone Creek, Reverend," he said to himself.

He and Serena hadn't been in their new home a full week, and already a crisis loomed. As usual, he handled it by slipping away for some quiet time with God.

He was more than six feet tall, but when he sat at the desk, he couldn't see out the small window just above his gaze. His view consisted of muted gold walls.

When he stood, he could peer into the tree-lined backyard filled with red and yellow roses. The flowers formed a lovely border along the perimeter of the white privacy fence that separated Micah and Serena's yard from their neighbors'. A spotlight cast a warm glow over them.

Instead of taking time to appreciate the view, Micah sat down again and put his hands behind his head. He leaned back in the chair and closed his eyes, trying to keep up with the questions racing through his mind.

Where was Erika? What had made her reach out to Serena now, after all this time? Was she still estranged from her alcoholic mother? Where was Elliott?

Micah knew he shouldn't expect answers anytime soon, but he was both heartened and saddened.

Erika had finally found the strength to leave Elliott, but it appeared she was in need of both emotional and spiritual support.

Serena had stopped unpacking after she received Erika's email and had spent the rest of the day trying to find her friend. First, she had replied to Erika's email—"Please call me or email me and tell me where you are. I want to help." Then she had begun making calls.

"Hello, I'm trying to track down a woman named Erika Wilson. She's petite and light complexioned, with gray-green eyes."

Serena launched into that spiel with the few women's shelters she was familiar with in the Richmond area, and even with the Virginia Family Violence Hotline, hoping that her position as executive director of a Richmond nonprofit agency would help her obtain some information.

Micah sat with her and rubbed her shoulders.

By ten o'clock she had called four shelters in the metro Richmond area and had no luck in finding someone willing to share information with her. She had checked her email again and found no response from Erika. The lack of success had left her near tears.

"This isn't working. I have to find her."

Micah thought about the contacts he had as pastor of Standing Rock Community Church. With a congregation of twenty-five hundred, there was bound to be a member with ties to the local domestic abuse prevention community.

"Don't worry," he told Serena as he continued to massage the kinks out of her shoulders and neck. "If Erika took the time to call Turner One and get your email address, she wants to talk with you. She'll contact you again."

Serena nodded. She and Erika, both only children, had been like sisters at one time. One was tall, the other short, one chocolate, the other honey, both beauty-queen material. One had struggled with her faith, while the other questioned whether there was a God.

Serena had always been the fun-loving, even-tempered member of the pair, while Erika had a feisty, go-getter attitude—except when it came to Erika's longtime love, Elliott.

Both of them had good hearts, and they had understood and loved each other. Even with all that had happened, it seemed their bond hadn't been permanently broken.

"You're right. She reached out to me," Serena told Micah. "When Erika's ready to be in touch, she will be."

Micah had convinced her to go to bed early so she would be well rested for their unpacking chores the next day.

Now, as Serena slept in their sleigh bed, he was ready to talk to God, or Daddy, as he and Serena sometimes referred to him. It had started soon after her mother died.

Serena had found herself at a crossroads with her biological father.

Serena had finally come to terms with the knowledge that while she had grown up believing Herman Jasper, her mother's deceased husband and the man listed on her birth certificate, was her dad, her father actually had attended church with her every Sunday. Her mother had revealed the truth a few years after Serena had completed college and was preparing for graduate school.

Melvin Gates, the esteemed deacon at the church Serena had grown up in, was really her father. Deacon Gates had wanted to help pay for grad school, but Serena wanted nothing to do with him.

In the four years since her mother's death, Deacon Gates had been making efforts to reach out to Serena. He had told his wife, two sons, and young daughter that he was her father.

Invitations for Sunday dinner and holiday gatherings had been extended. Deacon Gates occasionally called just to say hello.

Slowly and steadily, he and Serena had begun to form a friendship of sorts. Serena considered it that because, as she had told Micah, "The only father I've ever really had is God. He's been my Daddy through thick and thin. I'm not sure where Melvin and I are headed. Maybe one day I can consider him a father, but I'm not sure he'll ever reach Daddy status."

From then on, whenever Serena and Micah faced a difficult decision or discussed something weighty, Micah would lighten the mood with a sincere question: "Well, what's Daddy telling you, girl? He's the Man. What should we do?"

Micah called his own father, to whom he was very close, Pops. He enjoyed having such an intimate name for God, though. He felt like he was truly connecting with his heavenly Father when he could get on his knees and say, "Hey, Daddy, it's me again, coming to you for some direction and wisdom."

Tonight, as his wife slept, he uttered prayers for her friend Erika.

"You know exactly where Erika is and what she needs, Lord. That email today was no accident. Thank you for leading her to reach out to Serena. Help Serena, and me, to be there for her however she needs us to be. And wherever Elliott is right now, I lift him up in prayer too, asking that you lead him to you."

As Micah rose from his knees and sat back in his chair, he realized he was drained.

"A brother needs some sleep," he muttered.

He pushed himself up by his arms and crisscrossed through the boxes again.

He turned the light off in the office and stood in the doorway, peering toward his desk and out through the miniature window. The pie-shaped moon was in full view.

Even on a night as draining as this, God is in his glory, Micah thought. *He's going to see us through this, as always.*

Trust and believe. I AM.

"I hear you," Micah said aloud.

In this new house, with new hopes to begin a family and to reconcile with an old friend, he was reassured. When

Serena couldn't be strong, he knew he had to be, for her, and for himself.

With the changes he knew he had to make at Standing Rock Community Church, the road ahead wasn't going to be easy. He would need God to guide him and keep him focused. Wherever Erika was, she needed those same things.

6

Erika deleted the email from her mother and slouched in the uncomfortable chair.

"Lena, you are something else," she said under her breath.

And to think, people always said how much they looked alike. When they were together, strangers asked if they were sisters. As a child, Erika had loved the comparison. Then she had wised up.

She didn't want to be a doormat like her mother. She had decided she never would be. But look at her now.

"You look upset," a voice said from the doorway of the cubby-hole-sized office that held the shelter's two refurbished computers.

Erika looked toward the door and shrugged. "Hey, Charlotte. Disgusted is more like it."

Charlotte entered the room and pulled out the worn computer chair next to Erika. She sat sideways on the chair and leaned toward Erika.

"Want to talk about it?"

Erika closed her eyes and sighed. Since she had moved

into the shelter four weeks earlier, Charlotte Gregory had been an angel. Technically, Charlotte was the shelter's assistant director, responsible for administrative duties and arranging monthly programs for residents. In the short time Erika had lived there, she realized that for Charlotte, work meant more than just collecting a biweekly paycheck.

Charlotte had met Erika at Union Station the night Erika stepped off the train from Richmond after slipping away from Elliott. When Erika had arrived just before sunrise, the train station had been nearly empty. Still terrified that Elliott might have discovered she was gone, she had surveyed her surroundings with every step she took, as if she were a presidential secret service agent.

She spotted Charlotte immediately and, for some reason, was comforted by the woman's grandmotherly appearance.

Erika looked her way with a question in her eyes. Charlotte nodded slightly and offered a half smile. She was wearing the yellow parka Erika had been told to look for. She was a tall, full-figured, deep brown woman with the salt-and-pepper braids and half-moon glasses Erika knew her helper would be wearing.

As Erika cautiously approached her, Charlotte opened her arms and said in a booming voice, "How's my favorite niece? Come give Auntie a hug!"

Erika relaxed when she heard the phrases she had been told Charlotte would utter. She allowed Charlotte to envelop her in her thick arms and listened closely when Charlotte whispered in her ear.

"Erika?"

Erika squeezed her arm.

"You're safe now. Try not to look so nervous."

On the ten-minute ride to Naomi's Nest in the shelter's nondescript blue van, Charlotte didn't say much or ask many questions. When Erika began weeping, Charlotte hummed a song.

To this day, Erika didn't know what the melody was, but it had calmed her. When they pulled in front of the shelter, in northwest Washington, D.C., Charlotte removed the keys from the ignition and turned to her.

"We're here. Before we go in, would you like me to pray with you?"

"Um, no thanks," a startled Erika responded.

Had she unknowingly agreed to come to a Holy Rollers' place? Were they going to try to brainwash her into serving God?

Seeming to sense Erika's trepidation, Charlotte backed off.

"It's all right. Sometimes it helps soothe a client's nerves to pray before she has to go inside and fill out paperwork and answer so many personal questions, but there's no pressure—just something I offer everyone I have the opportunity to bring here for safety. I'm willing to pray with anyone at any time, because I know there's an abundant supply of God's grace and comfort."

Erika didn't reply.

Sounds like something Serena would say if she were here, she had thought.

Charlotte came around the van and opened Erika's door for her.

"Sandy, the night-shift shelter employee, called in sick. I'm working a fifteen-hour day to cover for her, but I don't

41

mind." Erika realized Charlotte was making light conversation to put her at ease. She spent the next hour in an intake session with Charlotte, disclosing details about her marriage she thought she would never share with anyone.

"Did the abuse occur regularly?" Charlotte asked without looking up from the form in her hands.

"Yes," Erika replied.

"Did you ever seek medical treatment for your physical injuries, and if so, how many times?"

"I was treated at least five times for broken bones or sprains. There were times when the pain was bearable, so I healed at home without going to the doctor."

Charlotte nodded, indicating that the pattern was familiar. The questions continued.

Yes, she had been forced on occasion to cancel activities or outings because her bruises would have been visible. No, she had never called the police. And yes, she still loved her husband.

"I know it sounds sick," she told Charlotte, too embarrassed to look her in the eyes. "I love him and yet I hate him. No—I guess I hate who he turns into when he starts to hurt me."

Erika raised her head.

"But last night I realized I was more tired of him than I was scared of him. It was like I realized I was drowning in my life."

Charlotte grasped her hand.

"I've been there, Erika. This is the first day of your journey to independence. Sometimes it's going to seem like you're not strong enough to make it on your own, but

42

you are. I'm along for the ride. Let me know if I can do anything to help you. Anything."

Charlotte meant what she said. Erika soon learned that Charlotte, a survivor of domestic abuse, led a weekly Bible study on Thursday evenings at the shelter. She also prayed individually with women who requested it, and yet she never forced her beliefs on anyone.

Like other women living in the shelter, Erika had quickly begun to trust Charlotte, but she still hadn't yielded to prayer and had avoided the Bible studies like the plague.

Charlotte never made her feel guilty or pressured; she always respected Erika's choices, even if she didn't necessarily agree with them.

"You've been forced into doing enough things by your abusive partner," she often told Erika and the other shelter residents. "I'm not going to take that route with any of you, for Bible study or any other activity that isn't mandatory."

As Erika sat at the computer this evening, she looked at Charlotte and shrugged. What difference would it make to talk with Charlotte about her self-absorbed mother? She wasn't sure why she had even tracked down the woman to share her new email address.

"If discussing it would help, I guess I would," Erika finally responded to Charlotte's offer to listen. "But nothing about my carefree and careless mother will change, not after all these years."

Charlotte smiled wryly.

"You're right—Mama ain't gonna change. But this really isn't about your mother, you know? What about Erika will change to accept this relationship as it is and move on?"

Erika turned off the computer, stood up, and stretched.

Just thinking about the drama she'd always had in her relationship with her mother made her head hurt. The empty place in the corner of her heart that had never been filled still echoed.

There was some good news, though. Serena had emailed her back. Even after all that happened, Serena still cared.

E, wherever you are, I'll come and get you. I want to help. All is forgiven. Please call me. The toll-free number at my job is 888-632-3333. Let me help you. I love you. Serena

After reading her mother's email, which had left her sad and tense, Erika hadn't found the heart to respond to Serena yet. She couldn't break the shelter rules and tell her friend where she was staying, and there were too many jumbled emotions wrestling for control to try to articulate them.

Sometimes she felt like a junkie in recovery—without the safety and support provided by Naomi's Nest, and the requirement to keep her whereabouts a secret, she might have been tempted to call her husband and see how he was doing. She might have melted at his whispers of love and decided to return home.

Whenever she had those thoughts, she resisted them. Staying at the shelter was the best way to ensure that she didn't act on them.

Maybe it was best to correspond with Serena just enough to let her know she was okay and would someday be in touch. Anything more might be dangerous for both of them. But it felt good, Erika realized, to know that someone besides her new friend Charlotte cared about what she was going through and wanted to help her.

Erika hadn't told her mother she had left Elliott and was living in a shelter. Mom was just crazy enough to call up Elliott and tell him what little she knew.

Even so, their insignificant correspondence had distracted her. She longed for a mother to whom she could tell the secrets of her heart and know they would be safe.

Bring them to me, my child.

The unbidden voice startled Erika, just as Charlotte's question about her willingness to change had. Was God speaking to her? She shook her head to discard the thoughts swirling inside. Living in this place was more than she had bargained for.

"I'm getting a headache. I think I'll go upstairs and lie down for a while," she told Charlotte.

Charlotte stood, and the two women left the small space together. Charlotte didn't seem fazed that Erika hadn't responded to the question about her relationship with her mother.

Charlotte turned toward her office as Erika strolled toward the shelter's foyer to climb the winding staircase. It led to the dorm-sized room she shared with a young mother and baby.

"You know, Charlotte, you could have been a shrink," Erika called out as she tackled the stairs two at a time.

Charlotte retorted with a challenge Erika wasn't ready to consider: "Bible study in thirty minutes!"

7

Serena grabbed the remote and turned off the DVD player. She picked up her towel from the gym mat and walked up the basement stairs into the kitchen.

As she wiped the sweat trickling down the back of her neck, her eyes scanned the countertops. Where had she laid it?

Micah took his eyes off of the game on ESPN and wiped his mouth with a napkin. He was relaxing in the great room, finishing off the ribs from their housewarming party the day before.

"Shaping things up?"

Serena whipped the white towel from around her neck and flung it across the room, knowing it wouldn't reach him. It landed in the arched opening between the great room and the breakfast nook.

"Be quiet and give me one of those ribs. I might not be skinny, but at least I'm saved, baby."

She had been moving to Donna Richardson's *Sweating in the Spirit* workout CD.

She searched the surfaces in the golden-hued kitchen again.

"Have you seen that printout from my email? I can't find it anywhere," she said, rifling through the stack of papers on the desk in the kitchen office nook. She wandered into the room where Micah sat.

Micah rose from the chocolate leather sofa, plate in hand, and approached his wife. He motioned for her to follow him into the kitchen.

"Don't know where it is," he said, "but I'll help you look."

He put the plate in the sink and grabbed a seat at the island, where he rested his chin in the palm of his hand. Serena watched him in disbelief.

"You call this helping?"

Micah grabbed her wrists and pulled her in closer.

"You stink, but you're still cute."

Serena smirked but leaned toward him. She smelled the barbecue on his breath but didn't mind. After three years of marriage, she fell in love all over again every time he peered into her eyes like he was doing right now.

It was a look that told her she didn't have to be perfect to earn his love. This look said he loved her simply because she existed.

Her heart pounding, Serena feigned irritation instead of kissing him.

"Who are you calling stinky?" she asked. "You've been out all afternoon playing basketball. The shower is calling your name."

Serena knew that Micah knew her well enough to recognize her game. She knew he'd make her pay later—on his terms.

"You're looking for the email you printed out from Erika, right? You've read it so much you should have it memorized. Why do you keep going back to it? You've emailed her back, now you have to be patient."

Serena rubbed her neck.

"I asked her to call me on the toll-free number at work. That was almost a month ago, and I haven't heard back from her at all. Maybe she said something in that email that will help me find her."

Micah pecked Serena on the lips. He grabbed her around the waist.

"You're not Sherlock Holmes, love. If Erika found enough courage to walk away from Elliott, she has to be relying on something other than her own strength, even if she doesn't see it that way yet."

Serena sighed.

"I just don't want her to suffer anymore. I know she's safer in a shelter where Elliott can't find her, but she's probably miserable, and here I am, living in what a lot of people would consider a dream home. It's not right. She's like a sister to me."

Micah swiped his thumb across her high cheekbones when she began to cry.

"It's OK to cry, but the most important thing you can do right now is pray, love. Just as Erika asked you to. Most shelters take care of food and clothing for their residents.

"And think about this: at least she's free from Elliott. That's worth a lot."

Serena nodded and looked down at her hands.

"I guess I'm also emotional because I'm still upset about my cycle coming last week. I'm not pregnant yet."

Pain pierced her heart like a dagger as she released the words. Micah hugged her tighter.

"*Yet* is the key word, Serena."

"I know, Micah, but what about the two ectopic pregnancies? Dr. Knott said it's difficult to predict whether I'll be able to sustain a pregnancy. We might spend all this money and have me undergo surgery to clear my fallopian tubes for nothing. Maybe I'm not meant to carry a baby."

Micah took her hands and looked her in the eyes.

"We'll cross that bridge if we come to it. Either way, God is going to bless us."

Serena nodded and wiped her still-damp eyes with the back of her hand.

"I know. Faith. Put it to work. Between Erika and baby worries, I'm a wreck. Where's that last rib?"

Micah pointed to his plate on the counter.

Serena licked her lips and sauntered over to it.

"Donna Richardson would be so disappointed in you. There's still some salad in the fridge."

"Mmm," Serena said as she picked up the rib and wrapped her lips around it. "Help yourself to the salad."

Micah laughed and approached her again.

"I have something better in mind. Let me help you work off that pork."

He took her hand and led her up the stairs. She wiped her mouth with the napkin she was still holding.

"Don't you have a sermon to finish?"

Ignoring her question, he paused on the landing to the

next flight of stairs and began crooning off key, "Let me hold you tight . . . if only for one night . . ."

Before Serena could beg him to spare her the crude Luther Vandross impersonation, the phone rang.

They hesitated. Micah shrugged, and Serena dashed to the kitchen to pick it up before the fourth ring sent the call into voice mail.

"It could be Erika," she said.

Micah rested his forearms on the wrought-iron banister and waited. Serena hung up and looked toward him.

"What?" he asked.

"Elliott says he's going to kill me if I'm keeping Erika away from him."

8

The music swelled and dipped as Serena and the other choir members swayed in their purple and gold robes to the mid-tempo beat. Brother Jared contorted his face and stretched his arms before him as if he were reeling in fish, urging the altos, sopranos, tenors, and baritones to sing from the center of their stomachs.

"I need more, more, more. Jesus, more of you," Tawana wailed into the microphone, her eyes lifted heavenward. "I need more, more, more. More of you."

The choir joined in with "More, more, more" as the Standing Rock Community Church congregation rose to its feet and lifted hands heavenward.

Micah approached the glass lectern and opened his Bible. He stood there, praying silently with his eyes closed as the choir completed the song, one of his favorites. He was thrilled that Tawana had taken a break from her studies at the University of Virginia to visit for the weekend.

When the choir members had taken their seats and the "Amens" had ceased, Micah surveyed the balcony and main floor of the sanctuary. Tawana's daughter, four-year-old Misha, and mother, Ms. Carson, sat in the third pew in the middle aisle, both gazing at Micah with reverence.

Besides the hard-of-hearing elderly woman who was flipping the pages in a hymnal and the fidgety younger children, everyone looked at him expectantly, including the teenagers, who were working overtime to appear disinterested.

Could he really preach another sermon on prosperity? *He who abides in Me, and I in him, bears much fruit.*

Micah heard God's voice, but still felt unsure. Was God telling him to preach this sermon as scheduled or disregard the trustees' wishes and preach what was really in his heart?

Micah cleared his throat and spoke to the waiting crowd.

"Good morning, Standing Rock! Let's give God some praise up in here!"

He turned toward the choir and clapped his hands. Serena, sitting on the third row in the soprano section, smiled at him and nodded slightly, her usual confirmation that she knew God was going to use him in a powerful way.

Micah turned back to the congregation and gripped both sides of the lectern. He led them in a brief prayer before announcing the message of the day.

"As your bulletins indicate, we are continuing the series 'Prosperity God's Way.' Just like God blessed Job, Abraham, David, and countless others who trusted in him, he is willing to grant favor to his children who walk this earth today. Open your Bibles and journey with me to the Word."

Micah hesitated as he gazed at the passage he had highlighted last night in the book of Mark, chapter 10. Rather than prosperity, it talked about how the desire to be great requires one to serve others.

Then he flipped to the text printed in the bulletin, Psalm 25:12–14. Intellectually, he knew there was nothing wrong or inaccurate about the sermon he was preparing to deliver—those who loved and feared the Lord would prosper.

Lately, though, God had been tugging at his heart to take Standing Rock members out of their comfort zones. They needed to be in the mission field, in the streets of the city, helping the hurt and the lost. Just last night a two-year-old girl had been killed in a drive-by shooting on the city's North Side.

Last week Micah had seen Jarvis, a thirteen-year-old boy who grew up in this church, working on one of the most notorious drug trafficking corners in the city. With his hands shoved in his blue-jean pockets, he had been surveying passing cars to determine whether a customer was ready to lock eyes with him. Jarvis had walked away when he realized the car pulling to the curb was his minister instead of someone looking for a hit.

With Jarvis on his mind, Micah returned his attention to this morning's message.

God blessed those who had a heart for him, Micah told his congregation. God gave to those who asked and did not waver in their faith. He had no problem with his children acquiring wealth and enjoying the finest things in life as long as they kept him first and wisely managed what they had.

Micah believed what he was saying. Look at how God

had led him to this church and had given him a wonderful wife and a beautiful new home.

Yet he also believed God blessed people so they could bless others. He knew there were people in his congregation who could help stem the tide of crime across the entire city, but especially in the struggling South Richmond neighborhood where the church was located.

They could help children and adults improve their reading skills. They could show young mothers how to bond with and nurture their babies. They could open a community kitchen and invite people who lived in the neighborhood to Sunday services or Bible study.

Instead, many members drove in from the suburbs on Sunday mornings and Wednesday nights and seemed oblivious to the stench of hopelessness and death that permeated the air. Micah couldn't keep his eyes and nose closed any longer.

It wasn't unusual on Sunday afternoons after church to find a group of glazed-eyed youths dressed in white T-shirts and blue jeans hanging out on the corner a block from Standing Rock, protecting their gang's turf. These were kids who should have been preparing for high school and college, for careers that utilized talents or gifts that had gone unnoticed and untapped. Standing Rock was just another building to them, though, not the haven Micah wanted it to be.

This morning as Micah preached the sermon the congregation was expecting, men and women rose to their feet and praised God for the blessings they had received and the blessings that were on the way. "Thank God *now* for the gift he's sending next week!" He glanced at the deacons and trustees on the front pews and saw they were beaming and shouting "Amen." As he wound to a close, the choir piped up with "God's Got a Blessing for You."

In the rear of the church, a scout from the Praises Go Up Gospel Network was standing and clapping. His sandy brown hair bobbed at his shoulders as he swayed to the fast-paced music flowing from the fingers and instruments of the guitarist and pianist. He nodded his head in approval and grinned as he observed the energetic congregation's reaction to the worship music.

Micah hugged a baggy-blue-jean-wearing teenager who came forward and told the congregation that he was seventeen and that his name was John Artis. Micah sent him to the side to talk with a church official. The choir continued to sing, and more people came forward as Micah walked the aisle and silently asked God to continue speaking to him.

Let me know, Daddy, what you want me to do. If this kind of preaching brings souls to your kingdom and you are satisfied, I will continue. If you want me to take another path, I will do what you desire, no matter what the church trustees say.

9

As Micah thanked the last worshiper for coming, Deacon Ames hobbled toward him with the PGU Gospel Network scout. Short and stout, with one leg longer than the other, Deacon Ames seemed, at first glance, to be in need of assistance. In fact, he was one of Standing Rock's most energetic and enthusiastic church leaders. His grandfather had chaired the trustee board at Standing Rock, and he figured it was only a matter of time before he secured the spot and continued his family's legacy.

"Great sermon today, Pastor," Deacon Ames said and slapped Micah on the back. "You were on fire! God is going to prosper you!

"This is Mr. Patrick Carter, the syndicated television network representative I was telling you about. He loved every minute of the service this morning. He wants to set up a meeting with us to talk about airing our eleven o'clock service on the network every Sunday!"

Deacon Ames was grinning so hard that Micah could see the PoliGrip securing his dentures. Micah turned and shook Mr. Carter's hand.

"Thanks for coming to the service. I'm glad you were blessed by it. Deacon Ames and some of the other church officials have mentioned that PGU has an interest in televising our sermons, and that's great. But of course, I'd like to get more information."

Patrick Carter smiled.

"I was here for the eight o'clock and the eleven o'clock services, and both were awesome. As we expand the network, we're looking for dapper young men like yourself to help us take our ratings to a new level. I like your style and your messages. You know how to set the people on fire!"

He laughed at his own turn of phrase.

"The people who watch PGU want to be given messages that inspire them, not all that fire and brimstone stuff."

Micah glanced at Deacon Ames, who was feigning ignorance. He had already talked to the deacons about ending his series on prosperity soon. What would PGU's interest mean for that plan?

Even as the question filled his head, Micah knew he couldn't worry about that. If he got caught up in trying to please not only the church leaders but also a TV network, he'd be traveling down a slippery slope.

Rev. Jones, one of his mentors in the ministry, had given him that advice the day he was installed as pastor of Standing Rock. As the two men had knelt in prayer in Micah's study, Rev. Jones had asked God to give Micah a pure heart.

When they rose to their feet and Micah put on his suit jacket, Rev. Tim Jones had grasped his shoulder.

"Son, if you don't remember anything else I tell you or

that I've tried to show you since your seminary days at Union University, remember this: This church isn't about you. You are the leader, but it ain't about you. You are here to let God channel his message and his will through you to his broken, hurting, and headstrong people.

"Leave the women alone, leave the money in the hands of the church officials, and don't try to win any popularity contests. The only one you need to be concerned about pleasing is the Lord.

"Now, you must show Christian love to your congregation, so don't be aloof and untouchable when they need you. But don't be so accessible that you're considered one of the boys or that the ladies don't respect your boundaries. You have to keep a sacred space for you and Serena. And most important, you have to make it a priority to keep talking to God and listening to him. If you don't, the demands and desires of everyone around you will drown out his voice. It can happen to the best of preachers."

Micah had gripped Rev. Jones's hand tightly and thanked him for the sound advice.

Today he remembered every word Rev. Jones had shared as he waved good-bye to Deacon Ames and Mr. Carter, who had exited through the front of the church and were descending the steps. He knew staying focused on that advice was critical right now.

Micah headed toward the church's administrative offices to find Serena.

Tawana, Ms. Carson, and Misha were waiting for him just outside the door to his study. Before he could say hello, Misha leaped into his arms and planted a juicy kiss on his cheek.

Micah's deep laughter echoed down the hallway as he chuckled heartily and hugged her tight.

"How's my favorite goddaughter?"

She leaned away from him and frowned.

"I thought I was your only goddaughter."

Micah laughed again as he put her down and gathered Tawana and Ms. Carson into a group hug.

"When did she get so smart?" he asked both women.

Tawana and Ms. Carson smiled at each other and shrugged.

"You should hear some of the things that little woman says," Ms. Carson said, beaming at her granddaughter. "When her mama is away studying, she keeps me company. It's like talking to another old lady."

Ms. Carson threw her head back and cackled at her own joke.

Ms. Carson had moved to Charlottesville with Tawana and had taken a job as a high school janitor. She helped care for Misha so Tawana could focus on her pre-law studies.

Micah turned to Tawana.

"Thanks for singing my song this morning, girl. You let the 'Lawd' use you!"

Now it was Tawana's turn to laugh.

"Does your congregation know how silly you are?"

At twenty years old, Tawana didn't look much different than she had at sixteen. But her countenance had changed.

Landing an academic scholarship to UVA had been life changing. She held her head higher and spoke with a confidence Serena and Micah hadn't known she possessed. No one had known she was a songbird until she joined the gospel choir at UVA on a challenge from her roommate, who didn't want to go to practice alone. Now people often paid her to sing in their weddings.

Micah shrugged at her question.

"Silly? Maybe not. But you've got to be touched in a special way to do this job. How's school going?"

Tawana's smile indicated that all was well, but before she could respond, Misha tugged at Micah's arm and looked up at him earnestly. With her large light brown eyes and thick sandy brown hair, she was the spitting image of her mother.

"Misha, I was just teasing," Micah said and scooped her up again. "You're my only godchild, my only girl."

Even as he said the words, he silently added *unfortunately*. He would give just about anything right now to hold a daughter of his own in his arms.

"Come on in," he said to the trio and opened the door to his study.

Serena was there with Aja, an eleventh grader who often came to her for advice. The girl reminded Micah of Tawana, and he was excited to have the chance to finally introduce them. Micah knew that Serena saw the same promise in Aja that she had seen in Tawana, despite the obstacles this girl was facing. Aja, shy and awkward around people she didn't know well, quickly excused herself from the reunion.

"Call me if you need to talk. Or better yet, stop by the Children's Art Coalition one afternoon, and we can chat while you help me with some work," Serena said and then rose to hug the willowy teenager.

Aja's close-cropped, layered haircut and thin frame gave

her an almost boyish appearance, but her high-wattage smile and perfect teeth transformed her bronze face into an image of femininity and magnetism. Micah and Serena were convinced the girl had a future as a model if she could avoid the neighborhood drug dealer who had decided he wanted her as his concubine.

Aja was afraid, and so was her mother. Serena had told her husband she was determined to help.

Aja softly bid farewell to everyone, including Micah.

"Have a good week, Pastor."

"You too, Aja. Take care."

Tawana and her mother stepped outside the study so Micah and Serena could gather their belongings and prepare to leave. Micah had offered to treat the ladies to dinner at Ma Musu's, a local Liberian restaurant that Tawana loved for its cornbread and melt-in-your-mouth baked chicken.

When they were alone, he gathered Serena in his arms. His muscles rippled through his suit jacket as he encircled her in his embrace and laid her head on his chest.

"You all right?" he asked her.

"Yeah," she answered softly. "Good sermon today, Reverend. I know God is going to bless us and keep us safe. And give us a baby or two."

Both of them still were unsettled by Elliott's call the night before. Serena had wanted to call the police, but since a lead detective on the force attended Standing Rock, Micah had contacted him instead.

Tommy Madson had been gracious enough to stop by the house and take the report himself.

"It's important to have this on file in case the calls continue," he had told Micah and Serena. "I'll ask the guys who cover this territory to patrol this neighborhood, and particularly your street, more often just to keep an eye on things."

Cops rarely had a reason to frequent Cobblestone Creek, so the promise had been reassuring to Micah and Serena.

"God has our backs," Micah said and kissed her forehead.

Serena looked up into his eyes.

"Did I ever tell you that the first time I saw you, the night I crashed my car into your Jeep, I was convinced you had to be related to Denzel Washington?"

Micah chuckled.

"Where did that comment come from, when we're standing here having such a spiritual moment?"

Serena smiled and shrugged.

"Who knows? I'm just glad I wasn't paying attention that night. What I thought was the worst thing at the time has turned out to be one of the best."

Micah gazed at her and shook his head.

"You're something else, lady. Let's go take our friends to dinner. When we get home, I need to fill you in on some things."

Serena feigned horror.

"You're not leaving the church, are you? I never got to wear my First Lady hats!"

Micah smirked.

"That was your choice—and a good one, I might add."

His expression sobered.

"The church has a major opportunity coming its way,

but God has laid a vision in my heart that might conflict with those plans. I just need you to join me in prayer about some things."

Serena squeezed his hand and picked up her purse.

"You got it."

10

Erika stepped off of the stool and stood back, hands on her hips, to survey her work. The burnt orange silk drapes she had wrapped loosely on a rod and hung over the single window in her bedroom added a surprising warmth.

Next to the window, on the scratched and wobbly mahogany chest of drawers she used to store her clothes, she had placed a trio of copper and orange candles of various heights.

Shelter rules forbade her from lighting them in her room, but they added a nice touch. Erika had purchased similar candles in cream and gold and set them on the dresser near her roommate's bed. Kathy would never admit it, but Erika knew she would appreciate the efforts to make their temporary living space more bearable.

Erika had found a framed picture of Pooh holding a pot of honey with ABCs engraved on the front for a dollar and couldn't resist buying it for Kathy's nine-month-old son. Xavier might not notice it, but Erika had asked Charlotte for permission to put a single nail in the wall and had hung the picture at crib level.

Her final touch had been to find gently used gold satin pillowcases. Erika had put one on her twin bed and the other on Kathy's. Their comforters were a deep red that had faded from repeated washings, but the pillowcases added a little kick.

Not bad, given what I'm working with, she thought as she surveyed her work.

For the first time since coming to the shelter over a month ago, Erika finally felt good about something. Just the simple effort of sprucing up her living space had lifted her spirits. For the first time since her arrival, she hadn't spent the afternoon wondering what Elliott was doing and whether he had forgotten about her. Despite her attempts to hate him, she couldn't.

Today she had dwelled on something other than her pitiful circumstances. She had joined other residents for a visit to a nearby Goodwill store.

Charlotte had rounded up women who would soon be leaving Naomi's Nest and had taken them on a shopping spree to search for items to decorate their new apartments or their living quarters in other long-term transitional shelter programs. Goodwill Industries gave the residents gift certificates that had been secured by donations from local Girl Scout troops.

As a new shelter resident, Erika wasn't qualified to receive a gift certificate to shop, but Charlotte had invited her along on the trip anyway. She liked Erika and had taken her under her wing.

"I can see through that feistiness, Erika," Charlotte had

said one afternoon when Erika had let down her guard and shared her doubts and fears. "You're a strong woman, but your spirit is fragile. You're human."

In her intake interview on the night she had arrived at the shelter, Erika had revealed to Charlotte how she had spent her days trapped in her five-bedroom home, reading recipe books and fashion or decorating magazines while Elliott worked. He had been so engrossed with appearances, with making sure everything looked just right and following the proper etiquette, that it had been a full-time job meeting with his approval.

Besides, Elliott hadn't wanted her out working or doing much else anyway. When she did shop, it was primarily via the Internet. The only excursions he approved of were the luncheons with other law firm partners' wives and her monthly tennis matches with the same group of women.

They had included her in the group for two reasons: Her beauty alone gave her the clout to move in their circles. Had she been in New York or L.A., she easily could have been a basketball wife or part of the Hollywood jet set. The group's more important reason was that as the wife of the only black lawyer with Benson Taylor Law, Inc., they had to keep her happy—until their husbands indicated otherwise.

Forays into their homes had exposed Erika to art and interior decorating that had taken her breath away. She had kept herself occupied by trying to make her home a beautiful haven too and, in the process, please her husband.

She hadn't realized that Charlotte had tucked that information away for future reference. She had been surprised by Charlotte's invitation to ride along to Goodwill, a store she hadn't visited since her days in high school, when she had lived hand to mouth with her nomadic mother. She had vowed never to return, but when she received Charlotte's request, she had found herself wanting to see what she could find when her day to leave the shelter eventually arrived.

Charlotte had driven the women to a Goodwill store in Rockville, Maryland, one of the wealthier suburbs of Washington, D.C., where the items the shelter residents found would be excellent in quality. Residents of the area, along with individuals who worked in the community, often donated clothing or other items with the tags still on.

As Becky, Tamara, Doris, and Evelyn searched for lamps, tables, and other necessities, Erika found herself drawn to the accessories. This certainly wasn't one of the posh stores she was used to patronizing, but she was excited to find silk curtains, candles, and knickknacks.

She had brought along fifty dollars of the money she had stashed away before she left Elliott and had spent twenty-eight dollars on the items she selected. Erika reined herself in because she knew her tiny room couldn't hold much more, but she was as giddy as a schoolgirl when she walked away from the register and went out to the van to tuck her bag in her seat.

After browsing through the clothing and deciding she didn't need anything, she wandered back over to the furniture section and found herself fingering a sturdy wicker plant stand with a wide base. It would be perfect for holding a fern or even a large framed photo.

She turned to Evelyn and Becky, who stood near her

struggling to decide on purchases for the apartment they would be sharing.

"Either of you like plants? This would be nice for your apartment. It's only five dollars."

Evelyn snorted dismissively.

"We don't have time to be buying beautiful stuff, Miss Prissy," Evelyn said in her raspy voice. Years of smoking had darkened her lips and deepened her register. "The basics will do."

"The donated bed, sheets, sofa, and chairs the shelter has helped you get are the basics," Erika retorted. "But they don't make a house a home."

Twirling a piece of her wavy auburn hair around her finger, Becky walked over to Erika and looked at the plant stand.

"We *are* moving on," she said softly as she ran the palm of her hand along the edges of the stand. "I'm ready to have some things in my life just because they're pretty. I'll get it with part of my gift certificate."

She smiled at Erika. "Any other ideas?"

By the time the women had boarded the van a half hour later, Becky had purchased the plant stand, a photo frame that complemented the stand, and books for her coffee table. She had also bought a purple and green table runner embossed with gold accents to match the donated deep purple suede sofa the table would be positioned near.

Erika had helped Tamara find a twin comforter for her fifteen-year-old daughter.

"She'll like the bright colors and the fact that it's feminine without being grown-up *or* childish," Erika had told her.

She had convinced Doris to buy a folding screen with

an Asian print to camouflage the volumes of books and magazines she had collected after fleeing her home. Erika had also helped her select a desk she could put in the corner to use for her quilting work.

"I'll help you sand it down and paint it once you're settled if you want," Erika had promised the beaming grandmother.

Erika had been so engrossed in helping her housemates that at first she hadn't noticed the tall, muscular man behind the cash register staring at her. When she helped Doris carry her purchases to the checkout counter, the man extended his hand to both women. He shook Doris's first.

"How are you today, ma'am? Find everything you need?"

Doris mumbled yes and averted her eyes as she searched for her gift certificate in her worn brown faux leather purse.

The man turned toward Erika and took her hand in his.

"And how are you?"

He didn't release his grip. Erika's hand felt child sized in his.

He looks like a professional bodybuilder, Erika thought as she turned red.

"Fine, thanks. We're ready to check out."

She politely removed her hand from his and waited for Doris to pay.

Before they left, the man smiled at Erika again.

"I don't know your name, but it has brightened my day to meet you. Maybe we'll cross paths again. I'm Derrick."

Erika gave a bitter laugh. If this man knew her circumstances, he would run like the air had been injected with the Ebola virus. She couldn't keep the sarcasm from spilling from her lips.

"If we meet again, I hope it will be during a happier time, in a better setting."

He cast her a questioning glance.

"Are you too bourgeoisie for Goodwill? It's a blessing that this place is here to help people in need—right?"

She thought about her purchases tucked away in the van and how excited she had been to find them. Shame filled her eyes. She couldn't look at him or Doris.

"You're absolutely right," she said softly. "I guess I'm taking this place and our meeting for granted. I'm Erika, by the way. Take care."

With that, she turned and strode quickly to the van, carrying one of Doris's bags. Doris was on her heels.

"He told you right, Erika. We shouldn't have contempt for a blessing. Just the little we've done today has made me feel better. I'm looking forward to a new beginning."

Erika turned and gave Doris a light hug. Had she really helped someone feel better?

"Thanks, Doris, I needed to hear that."

Charlotte, who had watched Erika from a corner of the store like a proud parent whose child was going off to college, was waiting for the women when they reached the van. Everyone else had boarded.

"You've got something there, Ms. Wilson," she told Erika softly. "Decorating may be your gift."

Erika glanced up at Charlotte curiously, surprised by the

admiration she saw in the older woman's eyes. Her own mother had never looked at her with such affection.

"You really think so? I was just giving my two cents' worth. It was fun."

Charlotte smiled and stood to the side, preparing to close the blue van door after Erika climbed in.

"That makes it even better."

11

Serena pulled her navy blazer tighter to her waist, then folded her arms as she walked up the slight incline to her car. Micah rested his hand in the small of her back and matched his stride with hers.

Their cars were parked, one in front of the other, about two blocks from La Grotta, the Italian restaurant in the historic Shockoe Slip section of downtown Richmond.

"It's turning cool early this year, isn't it?" Serena asked Micah.

He shrugged.

"It's late September, so it's not surprising."

When they reached Serena's faithful older-model Audi, she turned toward him and tilted her head up for a kiss. He leaned onto the car and gave her a long one.

"Have a good session with the kids," he told her and smiled into her eyes.

"You too," she said and laughed.

Micah was actually on his way to Standing Rock to meet with church officials and Patrick Carter about the contract the Praises Go Up Gospel Network had drafted to nationally televise the church's eleven o'clock worship service.

Micah had met with Patrick two weeks ago about the opportunity and had been praying ever since for God to give him wisdom on what to do.

"What's the problem?" Serena had asked when he shared details about the situation with her. "You'd be expanding your ministry, sharing God's Word with more people. Isn't that a good thing?"

"Not if the Word has to be choreographed or dictated by the network or by Standing Rock church officials."

His jaw had been firmly set, letting Serena know he felt strongly about his position.

"If I happen to preach on prosperity, so be it. But if God lays it on my heart to preach about serving others or salvation or tithing, that has to be okay too. From my conversation with Patrick Carter, I sensed that the network is looking for a formulaic approach to keep viewers coming back each week, revved up, and feeling like they're doing all right. I ain't for all that unless that's what God wants."

Serena had walked over to the leather recliner where he sat that night holding the remote control but not really paying attention to ESPN. She had stood next to him and cradled his head against her flat belly, wishing she were carrying his child.

"I feel you, babe. I'm with you, whatever you decide."

Tonight's meeting was going to be interesting. If the contract dictated what Micah would be required to preach and teach on Sundays, he wasn't going to sign. Serena knew there might be some shouting, some pouting, or worse in that closed-door session.

"Should I not wait up for you tonight?" she asked.

"Probably not, love. You be careful going into the house, okay? I'm going to run; the meeting starts in twenty minutes."

He opened the car door for Serena and closed it before striding to his Jeep, parked behind her car. Every year the church offered to lease him a newer model car, but Micah always insisted that the money be used to fund programs for youths and senior citizens in the church and in the community. So far efforts to do community outreach had been lackluster.

Serena's Children's Art Coalition session with the youths living at the Emergency Shelter, Inc., on Franklin Street was just ten minutes away. Since she had a few extra minutes, she decided to call Aja to make sure the girl still planned to meet her there tonight to volunteer.

Micah pulled away and waved as she scrolled through her PDA to find Aja's number. She told herself for the tenth time that tonight she was also going to program the digits into her cell phone so she wouldn't keep having to search.

When she had found the number, she quickly dialed it and held the minature cell phone to her ear. It rang several times before going into voice mail.

A good indication that Aja was on her way, she decided.

Tap, tap, tap.

Serena heard the light knocking on her window as she tucked her cell phone and PDA into her purse.

She turned to find a pair of wild eyes boring into her. Elliott's.

Thank God she had locked the door. Micah had just turned the corner, and no one else was traveling this stretch of road.

He tapped on the window again and began yelling.

"Serena! Where is she? I need my wife back!"

Serena's eyes widened. She remembered her keys in her lap and fumbled as she sought to find the ignition key.

"Stop ignoring me! Let this window down!"

He stood there, clean shaven and more handsome than she had remembered, in a custom navy suit. He was a picture of professionalism and success. What Serena saw in Elliott's tortured gaze, however, was anger and humiliation.

Her gut told her that if he got his hands on Erika, he would kill her. She wasn't too sure the same fate didn't await her.

Since she couldn't find the key, she summoned the courage to talk to him. Maybe if she could calm him down, he would leave.

"Elliott, take it easy," she yelled through the glass separating them. "I haven't talked to Erika since before Micah and I got married. I don't know where she is. I have no idea."

Serena held her breath and rationalized her comments. Emails didn't count as talking. She longed for the day she *would* talk to her friend again.

She reached into her open purse on the passenger seat while keeping her gaze on Elliott, praying that she could grab her cell phone without him noticing.

At that moment a car turned onto Twelfth Street and slowed as it approached her Audi. The freckled-faced man behind the wheel tapped his horn and waved.

A scowling Elliott took his gaze off Serena and transformed his facial expression in seconds.

"Forest! How are ya, man?" Elliott grinned broadly and waved back. "How's your case going? I'm taking files home tonight to do more research, after I help my wife's best friend here get her car started."

Elliott looked at her like she was his favorite cousin.

"Try it again, Serena. I'm betting the battery is weak. You probably left the inside light on."

Forest glanced at her and nodded hello.

"Need me to help?" he asked Elliott. "I don't know much about cars—our family mechanic does everything from changing the oil to washing them. But I could get him on the phone for some advice."

Elliott continued his farce.

"Don't trouble yourself. I already called the office and had my new assistant, Douglas, give AAA a call to bring booster cables. Her car should start now with no problem. See you at the office tomorrow?"

Forest smiled and waved again before pulling away in his silver Mercedes coupe.

Serena sat there, stunned by the interaction. Why hadn't she spoken up and told the guy she needed help?

I will never again watch another horror movie and blame the victims for standing there wide-eyed and helpless instead of running.

Forest had provided a helpful distraction, though. She had finally located the right key. As she inserted it in the ignition, Elliott crouched near Serena's car door and looked in her eyes. She realized that he had been going to work pretending that life was normal and trying to cover for his wife's absence. At night, though, he would go home to an empty house and lose it.

Serena was surprised by a sudden surge of sympathy. This jerk had been beating her best friend for years, since their days at Commonwealth University. Thank God Erika had grown tired of the abuse and had finally left him.

Love doesn't hold grudges. He is your brother.

Elliott? she thought. *Okay, Lord, I hear you, but this is stretching it. I'm going to need your help with this one.*

For the first time since their long-ago meeting, however, she saw Elliott for the insecure, unhappy person he was. If he could have dealt with his issues in some other way, instead of taking them out on the woman who loved him, he could have been a good guy.

When you refuse to help the least of these, you refuse to help me.

Serena pressed the button and slightly opened her window. She tried to keep her voice from quivering.

"Elliott, I'm about to drive away now, because someone is waiting for me and will get worried if I don't show up. I don't know where Erika is. I don't know what happened between you two, but I do know what used to happen. If you want her back, you've got to make some changes. That's all I can say."

Her words took the fight out of him. He looked at her listlessly and backed away from the car.

"If you talk to her, tell her to come home," he said

solemnly, trying to hold back tears. "I'll do whatever she wants."

Serena started the car and pulled away from the curb, shaken by the fact that he had apparently followed her and had been watching her, waiting for Micah to leave.

Elliott, who stood there looking pitiful as she drove away, had made those promises before. She didn't believe him now any more than she had when he had started abusing Erika in college.

He had never given her a reason to trust his word. Wherever Erika was, she must be feeling the same.

12

Dear Serena, Sorry it has taken me so long to reply to your email. Life here in the shelter is unusual. I have my good days and bad days, days where I doubt that leaving Elliott was the right decision and days where I'm certain it was. Thank goodness he hasn't found me.

Has he been bothering you? Even though we haven't talked in years, he knows you were the closest friend I had, so I'm sure he'll try to contact you. Please be careful. He can get mean when he can't have his way.

Serena, I wish I could tell you where I am, but it would put both of us in danger, and I would be kicked out of here. There's nothing you can do for me now but pray. (Yes, I said pray. I'm finally learning how to do that.)

I am in a safe place where there are people who care enough to help me get on my feet. One lady in particular, I'll call her "C," is like a mother to me—more than my own mother ever was. She has been wonderful.

I'm not sure when I will see you again. But just knowing that you have forgiven me and that you are thinking about me and pulling for me helps me to go on. You could have washed your hands of me a long time ago when I refused to respect your faith or leave Elliott at your urging. I know now how stupid I was on both counts. I'm still not sure what this faith thing means to me, but my friend here, "C," leads a regular Bible study. I have refused to go since moving here, but tonight I'm going to give it a try.

I found out something yesterday that brought me to my knees. The only thing that can help me through this has to be the God you love so much. I am pregnant. E

Before she changed her mind about sending the email, Erika clicked the mouse.

She inhaled deeply to smother the cry that wanted to escape. The tissues she had been carrying in her pocket all day were gone. She should have been cried out by now, but every time she thought about that positive pregnancy test, a fresh waterfall erupted.

How on earth was she going to care for a baby? She had little money, an expired realtor's license, and no place to call her own. Was this a sign that she should go back to Elliott?

If she went back and told him she was pregnant, maybe he wouldn't hurt her, for the sake of the baby. She realized that wasn't likely. If she had to shut down her emotions to endure the abuse, what could she rely on to be a good mother? She hadn't had an ideal role model, so she had no clue what proper parenting entailed.

The more Erika thought about it, the sicker she became.

When she had begun to feel nauseous last week, she had suspected the flu or a virus. Sharing a room with a mother and baby made her prone to catch Xavier's sniffles and illnesses.

She had vomited just before a house meeting with the shelter staff. Charlotte had found her in the bathroom across the hall from her bedroom. Erika had flushed the toilet and was clinging to the wall.

Charlotte helped her to her bed and tucked her in.

"You don't have a fever. Could you be pregnant?"

Erika's last night with Elliott flashed across her mind. That had been about seven weeks ago.

"Yes, I guess I could be," she said weakly. "But please don't say that."

Charlotte left the room and returned with a home pregnancy test. The shelter was equipped for all kinds of emergencies.

"You want to do this now or later? It's best for you to know for sure."

Erika stared at the box for the longest time without responding. She had to be dreaming. She had left her home and husband, thinking she was free, and now she could be pregnant with his child. She wanted to know now.

When she emerged from the bathroom holding a tester that showed two blue lines, indicating a positive result, her face said it all. She had collapsed in Charlotte's arms and wailed.

"What am I going to do? I can't do this. I'm scared!"

After the tears had abated, Charlotte sat on the twin bed with Erika and grasped her hands.

"Oh, child, I hope you don't have a permanent dent in this mattress when I get up," she said and laughed. "I look good, but I *am* a big girl."

Erika smiled through the tears coursing down her face, thankful for a few seconds of comic relief. Charlotte, still clutching Erika's hands, grew serious.

"When I left my husband after eleven years of marriage

in 1988, I came to this very shelter with an infant, a three-year-old, and six-year-old twins.

"The other women living here thought I'd lost my North Carolina mind. There was no way a single woman was expected to raise four children by herself and be self-sufficient back then. They questioned just how bad the abuse had been, why I hadn't been able to take it."

Charlotte shook her graying braids at the memory and gave a half laugh.

"It's so easy for others to look at your circumstances and tell you what you need to do. They didn't realize that they were in my same predicament, whether they had one child or none. Each of us was trying to free ourselves from someone's grip. Each of us had been 'searching for love in all the wrong places,' as the song says.

"It took me a while, Erika, and it wasn't easy. I got a job that paid for me to return to school and went part-time for seven years to get a master's degree in social work. I bought a home. I learned how to love myself.

"So please, trust God that it's going to be all right. He really doesn't give us more than we can bear."

Erika sniffled and looked at Charlotte.

"What if I've never believed in God before? My mother and third stepfather, a chronically unemployed professor, drilled into me the notion that religious folks were fanatical and uneducated. I believed that until I met my friend Serena. But even she didn't erase all my doubts. What makes you think God will help me?"

Charlotte smiled. Her full, pecan-hued cheeks made her eyes crinkle.

"None of us is worthy of God's love, Erika. We all sin

and fall short of his expectations. We're imperfect, and he loves us anyway."

For the first time, Erika wanted to know more about this merciful God. She didn't ask Charlotte any questions, though. There was a lot to digest.

Instead, she hugged the woman and asked to be excused from the shelter meeting in progress downstairs. The twenty other women living in the house were already there.

"I need some time to think."

Erika had tossed and turned all during that night. Her toddler roommate, Xavier, had made matters worse. She knew it wouldn't be long before she found herself in a predicament similar to Kathy's.

She had awakened in the middle of the night and padded downstairs to the pay phone in the hallway off the kitchen. It had been dark, but she used the miniature flashlight on her key chain to light up the dial pad.

What would Elliott say if she called him and told him she was pregnant? Would he change and seek help so they could be a family?

She had picked up the receiver and pressed zero to make the collect call.

"What is the number, ma'am?" the operator had intoned.

Erika had frozen. She couldn't do this. The pay phone number would show up on the caller ID, and Elliott would be able to find her. If she told him she was having his baby, he'd have a reason to hunt her down, whether she wanted to be found or not.

She had replaced the receiver and slumped against the

phone, holding herself as the tears fell. When she had climbed back into bed, she curled into a ball and covered her head with the thin comforter.

How did one talk to God? She had softly recited the only prayer she knew, a childhood grace she had learned years ago in a summer camp program.

"God is great. God is good. Let us thank him for our food . . ."

Erika thought about that prayer tonight, a week after finding out she was pregnant. Tonight she was going to get some questions answered, and maybe she'd even learn another prayer.

She kissed her fingers and touched them to the screen as the email she had sent Serena floated into cyberspace. She rose from the computer chair and turned off the light on her way out of the room.

Bible study began in ten minutes. She wanted a front-row seat.

13

Serena called Micah from her cell phone as soon as she turned off Twelfth Street and drove east on Main Street toward the shelter where she'd be conducting a program tonight. His phone went right into voice mail. He'd probably turned it off so he could pray on his way to the meeting at church.

Serena felt the need to talk to God—Daddy—too.

Thank you for keeping me safe tonight.

She hesitated and rolled her eyes while slowing for a red light.

I guess I need to pray for that crazy Elliott too. Help him in the way only you can.

She listened to Micah's voice mail greeting before leaving a brief message.

"Hey, call me as soon as you can. When you drove off tonight to get to your meeting, Elliott showed up and tried to force me to tell him where Erika is. I'm okay, and I'm going on to the shelter to work with the kids. But I'm a little nervous about going into the house alone.

"I'm going to call Tommy Madson and see if he or another officer can escort me inside. I know your meeting is important, so don't worry about leaving early. I'll be fine. I just wanted to let you know. Love you."

By the time Serena reached Emergency Shelter, Inc., she was calmer. She had talked to Detective Madson, and he had agreed to meet her in front of her house at nine o'clock.

She took a few more deep breaths and prayed for God to help her focus. Right now she wanted to concentrate on reaching into the hearts of these special children.

About a dozen first through fifth graders crowded around her as she walked through the door of the shelter and headed for the recreation room, carrying a clear container of supplies. The recreation room was located in the rear of the eighty-year-old building that had once served as home to a well-to-do Richmond family.

"Hi, Mrs. McDaniels! Did you bring the paint? Did you remember my markers? What are we doing today?"

Several youngsters talked at once. Some grabbed her waist as she walked by.

"Guys! Girls!" Serena yelled over the commotion. "Let me get settled and I'll answer all of your questions. Are Miss Aja and Miss Kami here?"

Paris's three ponytails bobbed at her shoulders when she nodded. Just five years old, she was precocious and precious.

"Both of the big helpers are here, Ms. Serena. They're in the art room, putting paper on the tables and taking out the art aprons."

Serena paused and squatted to give the tiny girl a hug.

Paris could pass for a child a year younger, but when she talked she seemed much older. Living on the streets and moving from house to house with her mother had taught her more than she needed to know about life at her age.

For a couple of hours twice a month, Serena and the art coalition volunteers brought out the kid in Paris and the other youngsters living in the long-term shelter with their mothers. For a few hours each week, the children got a chance to express their hopes and dreams on paper, through drawing, painting, and sometimes writing.

When they shared their drawings of the kinds of houses they wanted to someday own, Serena encouraged them.

"You can have that and more, as long as you have faith in yourself and work hard to reach your goal," she would tell them.

She was touched when the children would draw her picture and say they wanted to be like her or marry someone like her someday.

"You're tall like a skyscraper, as nice as my first-grade teacher, sweet as a chocolate ice cream cone, and smart enough to be president. I think I love you!"

Serena had framed that note from eight-year-old William, who it turned out was a budding artist and writer. She had convinced a professional artist who volunteered with the Children's Art Coalition to give the boy private art lessons at no cost. The artist had been so impressed that she paid for him to attend one of the summer art sessions offered for children at the Virginia Museum of Fine Arts.

Now the once-sullen, chubby Hispanic boy was thriving in school and had become focused on someday seeing his work displayed in galleries.

Serena dumped her supplies on the long white table in the center of the art room and was finally free of little hands as the children rummaged through the pile to secure markers, crayons, glue, and scissors for their projects.

She looked toward the opposite end of the room, where Aja and Kami stood chatting, the children's art aprons draped across their arms.

"Hey, ladies. Thanks for coming out tonight."

Aja smiled shyly. Art wasn't one of her strengths, but Serena realized that helping these children, whose circumstances weren't that different from Aja's own, made her feel better.

Kami, cheerleader perky and thick in a way the young men loved, strolled over to Serena with her arms outstretched for a hug.

"How've you been? Dad told me to tell you hello."

Serena smiled at her half sister, who was now sixteen and a high school sophomore, attending the Governor's School. Serena remembered the night she had called Melvin Gates's home and confronted him with the truth: he wasn't just a deacon at her church—he was her father.

Young Kami had been in the background asking for a bedtime story. Serena had been jealous. Melvin had been evasive.

Now he sought to embrace his truths, which included asking his family to accept Serena. Kami had been stunned and hurt that her father, who she thought could do no wrong, had been unfaithful to her mother. For more than a year, she had remained aloof, even though Melvin still lived at home and was in counseling with his wife.

Serena also knew that Althea Gates had worked through her anger and grief about her taken-for-granted trust in her husband. A year after the death of Serena's mother, and a year to the date that Melvin had shared the truth with her, Althea had sat down with Kami and her two sons, James and Perrin, and told them she was forgiving their father and recommitting herself to her marriage.

She had asked them to release their grudge against their father, who had left home for a round of golf at her request.

Kami had been thirteen at the time, but Althea later told Serena that she felt Kami was old enough to hear the truth, to understand how life sometimes unfolds, so she could make better choices.

"What happened nearly three decades ago is over," Althea had told Serena over lunch soon after that meeting with her children. "Melvin stayed with me, Kami joined our family, and now we have you to welcome into the fold. You didn't do anything wrong. You have the right to get to know your father. And your siblings."

With her mother's blessing, Kami had treated Serena as a sister ever since.

Serena wasn't sure if it was because Kami was so young or so sincere, but she treasured her relationship with the girl—more than the strident attempts Melvin had made to carve a place for himself in her life.

Monthly lunch dates had given Serena and Melvin opportunities to get to know each other better and to become comfortable with each other outside of church.

Sometimes he invited her to dinner with the family, which she still found awkward, given her high school crushes on what were now her half brothers. And Melvin occasionally visited Standing Rock to hear Micah preach.

Serena was polite and chatted with him as she would a colleague with whom she was friendly, but they never delved beneath the surface.

The formalness of their relationship made her uncomfortable. While they got along well, Melvin didn't really know her.

He knew she had made peace with her past after Mama's death, but she hadn't told him she and Micah were struggling to conceive. He knew very little about Erika and her abusive husband. He wasn't aware of Micah's conflict with Standing Rock leaders.

Melvin had been excited when Kami and Serena had grown close. When Serena had switched jobs, Kami had been one of the first volunteers to work with her at the Children's Art Coalition.

Serena had been touched. Now the children they worked with were enthralled.

They loved having not only Serena but also Kami and other young volunteers like Aja shower them with the attention they craved. Their moms were so busy scrambling to find work and become independent enough to leave the shelter that tenderness was the last thing on their minds, if it was there at all.

Who had time for hugs and kisses when children needed to be toughened up just in case they had to live on the streets again? Many of these mothers felt that way, the shelter director had informed Serena.

Serena stood near the easel tonight after giving instructions on the weather-related pictures she wanted the children to draw. She watched Kami cuddle with Paris and a sandy-haired boy named Leon and silently thanked God for blessing her with this job and with a sister.

Who would have believed I would be spending quality time with Deacon Gates's other daughter? she thought.

Serena recalled Elliott's frantic efforts earlier tonight to bully her into revealing information she didn't have about Erika. She thought about her consistent prayers to have a baby and, eventually, a brood of her own children surrounding her with hugs and playfulness.

Life had so many twists and turns that the journey couldn't help but be eventful, she thought. And sometimes painful.

She still missed her mother deeply. Serena knew Mama would have understood her longing to have a baby that resembled her. Mama had tried for years to conceive, only to become pregnant with Serena when her relationship with her husband was strained and she sought comfort in Melvin Gates's arms.

Would Serena ever be the guest of honor at a baby shower instead of always a guest? Did she even have the right to feel this way?

Trust in my timing and in my ways. I am your Father. I know what's best for you.

Serena knew those promises were true, but her arms ached from emptiness right now.

14

Micah sat at the head of the long oak table and examined the expressions on the faces of the twenty-one men and women on Standing Rock's deacon and trustee boards.

Patrick Carter was wrapping up his presentation on the benefits of featuring Standing Rock's services on the Praises Go Up Gospel Network.

"Not only will ten million viewers across America have an opportunity to watch and support your ministry, but so will at least two million people overseas, in countries like Turkey and China, where Christian television is slowly filtering onto the airwaves.

"You'll be asked to pay a standard syndicates membership fee of ten thousand dollars a month, but that can be taken from your earnings and from the funds you receive from people who send in donations to the ministry."

Micah leaned forward and interrupted.

"So you're saying we have to beg viewers for money to stay on the air?"

Patrick laughed nervously and wrung his hands.

"I wouldn't use the word *beg*, Reverend," he said. "They can become your partners or send in love offerings, or what we call 'gifts of the Spirit.' Everybody has their own way of doing it."

Deacon Ames, whose eyes had been glued to Patrick Carter, turned toward Micah and frowned.

"He's right, Pastor. It's no different than collecting an offering on Sunday morning. Our members—and our regular television viewers—should contribute to the upkeep of the ministry."

Micah shrugged and sat back in his seat. He'd have to pray on this one—and do some research.

"Sorry to have interrupted. Continue."

Patrick resumed his speech, emphasizing that the benefits of televising the church services would yield invitations for the church choirs to travel and possibly record a CD and for Micah to be invited to preach before prominent congregations across the country.

"When Christians have a weekend stay in Richmond, Virginia, they'll make a point of seeking out Standing Rock. That will help your offerings and your congregation grow by leaps and bounds."

Patrick paused to see if there were questions before continuing.

"Because Standing Rock will be the PGU Gospel Network's newest addition, you will not receive a prime-time slot. That is given to the shows with the highest ratings. Initially, Standing Rock's services will air on Sundays at 11:00 p.m.

"We evaluate ratings every quarter and update show air times and listings every spring and fall. Based on how well the show does in the ratings, you could move to an early Sunday morning time slot or to the window between 5:00 and 10:00 p.m., which contains our prime evening slots."

Beverly Grady, the church's caterer and granddaughter of one of Standing Rock's now-deceased pastors, raised her hand.

Micah smiled inwardly. Putting her on the church's finance committee had been a wise decision. When it came to Standing Rock's fiscal matters, Sister Grady, who was usually demure, became as hard-nosed as a CIA interrogator.

"What you're saying is we have to pay to be on your network? And you're saying the best way to come up with this money is to beg strangers to give it? And you're saying we'll be on late Sunday night, when people my age are fast asleep? Shoot, I won't be awake to watch what I'm paying for."

She leaned forward in her seat, her ample bosom pressing against the table. She arched one of her well-maintained brows.

"You've told us how all of this will benefit Standing Rock. What's in it for the PGU Gospel Network? The $120,000 we'll be paying you?"

Patrick smiled and looked toward Deacon Ames for support. But even Deacon Ames had sense enough not to cross Sister Grady. He smiled and clenched his lips together, as he always did when he was trying to tighten his dentures.

Patrick tried to respond.

"Well, now, it depends on how you—"

Sister Grady interrupted.

94

"The more I think about this, I'm not seeing this as a win-win situation. Would Standing Rock be able to do this on a trial basis without paying the fee, say thirty or sixty days, to make sure it's a good fit?"

Patrick considered the question.

"I'm not sure that's possible. We never like to start a show and then abruptly pull it; and besides, it takes a while to build a following. Standing Rock would need to air weekly for at least six months for us to determine whether the show works for our network.

"Based on the worship services I've attended, though, I can assure you that won't be an issue. These days people are flocking to churches that teach them how to prosper and live the abundant life. They're hungry for that kind of message. Trust me, this church can easily bring in thirty-five hundred dollars a month in revenue solely from the TV ministry. The ten thousand dollars will seem like a small sacrifice once you're up and rolling."

He continued, speaking directly to Sister Grady.

"I can get this committee copies of quarterly reports from the past two years that show how other churches that started out with the 11:00 p.m. time slot soon found themselves thriving."

Deacon Ames grinned at him and at the rest of the board members, most of whom had been reeled in from the moment they heard "national TV" mentioned in the same sentence as "Standing Rock." Micah's assistant pastor, Jason Lyons, was on board too.

Sister Grady seemed satisfied. She sat back in her chair and relaxed.

Micah still wasn't convinced. He held up his copy of

the tentative contract Patrick had brought along for the deacons and trustees to review.

"You say viewers like messages on prosperity, and I see that you have a prominent reference to Standing Rock's commitment to the 'prosperity gospel' in this document. What happens if I decide to completely change the focus of my messages?"

Before Patrick could respond, Deacon Turner jumped in.

"Why would you, Pastor? If this is going to take us where we need to go, why stop now? God has obviously opened this door."

Micah looked at Jason, hoping another preacher could relate to the need to remain open to God's guidance. Jason shrugged as if to say he had no opinion in the matter.

Surprised, Micah paused.

What's that about?

He gathered his bearings. He would hash things out with the board when their guest left, but he needed to know, for the record, what the contingencies of this contract were.

"I've never considered Standing Rock a prosperity gospel ministry. I've spent the past eight weeks preaching on prosperity and will do so for another two, because that's the series God gave me to share with the congregation," Micah said. "Once that's done, there are other messages our church family needs to hear to keep maturing in our faith and service."

Silence engulfed the room. Sister Grady shifted her eyes away from Micah and toyed with the diamond bauble on her right hand.

Jason squirmed in his seat and opened his Bible.

Deacon Ames glared at Micah.

Patrick cleared his throat and responded.

"PGU is looking for a church with a particular type of ministry to fill this available time slot. If you don't feel Standing Rock fits the description in the contract, then maybe we need to reevaluate our offer."

Deacon Ames vigorously shook his head. He rose from his seat and walked over to Patrick, who at six feet four, stood a foot taller than him.

"Mr. Carter, we know this is a great opportunity. Please don't be discouraged by the questions raised in tonight's meeting. We're going to go into our executive session now to discuss this further. I'll escort you out, and we'll be in touch soon."

Patrick nodded.

"I certainly understand. You can reach me on my cell phone if other questions arise as you continue the meeting. I'm heading back to my hotel and will leave for Maryland tomorrow morning around ten o'clock."

He turned to address the committee and grab his briefcase from the table.

"Thank you all for having me here tonight. I hope I've convinced you to accept this once-in-a-lifetime opportunity. Not only will this make Standing Rock Community Church legendary, it will help save souls.

"If you decide to join with us, we need to move forward as quickly as we can. We'll need a signed contract by the first of the year to prepare for a late winter or early spring launch of your broadcast. If that's not doable, we won't be able to get you on the air until summer. Blessings to you all."

The committee members bade him good-bye. He waved to Micah and followed Deacon Ames out of the conference room.

The group began murmuring as soon as the door closed.

"What do you think?"

"I think we should go for it!"

"Why is Pastor so uptight about this?"

"It's time to move into the twenty-first century."

"We should be flattered that a television network is interested in us."

Micah heard the under-the-breath chatter but sat silently with his arms folded until the committee members settled down.

Sister Grady was the first to raise a question.

"Pastor, you know I have my reservations when it comes to spending money, but it sounds like this opportunity could bless our church greatly. Why are you so concerned about the focus of the message? Are you afraid you'll run out of things to preach about?"

She had been one of his biggest supporters when he was hired to lead Standing Rock four years ago. She always told him the truth and had been a real friend to him and Serena.

Micah respected and loved her, but even she couldn't sway him on this one.

"Sister Grady, I'm not afraid of coming up with sermon topics. I'm afraid of being beholden to a contract instead of to God."

Deacon Ames slid back into the room before Micah continued. He glared at Micah as he took his seat.

"You almost messed us up, Pastor. I smoothed things over."

Micah continued without acknowledging Deacon Ames's comments. He stood and waved a copy of the *Richmond Times-Dispatch* in the air.

"See this front-page article? Another young black man has been killed on a street near this church. He was fourteen and went astray after his mother died. The police think his murderer is a fifteen-year-old boy who was seeking revenge for a drug debt."

Blank stares greeted his passionate comments.

"This is the fiftieth death in the city this year. Over half of those who were murdered were under age eighteen.

"I'm fine with Standing Rock being televised nationally, but I'm more concerned about reaching the lost and the angry and the unsaved right here at our doorstep.

"How can we spiritually bless the masses we may never know except through television when we won't take the time to reach out to the people right around us who need bread, water, and spiritual food?"

Deacon Turner rolled his eyes.

"If they'd get jobs, they could eat," he said in his characteristic Alabama drawl.

Deacon Ames grunted.

"When did you decide to become the savior of Richmond's downtrodden people?"

Deaconess Melba Pugh was more diplomatic.

"Pastor, there's a saying, 'If you always do what you've always done, you'll always get what you've always gotten.' This seems like a wonderful opportunity to do something powerful at Standing Rock. I hope you're not letting fear get in the way of progress. I don't have a problem with preaching on prosperity, because we can learn so much from that. It's relevant to every aspect of our lives, from our finances to our relationships. It's all in how you look at it."

Micah smiled at Deaconess Pugh. Her deep faith often startled people who usually focused on her elegant demeanor. She was a diva with a capital *D*, but she had no problem letting people know that G-O-D came first.

Lord, am I wrong? Am I operating out of fear? Am I making a foolish power play?

Deacon Ames interrupted Micah's internal dialogue.

"Look, Pastor, I've always respected you and your decisions, but I think you're heading down the wrong road with this one. What does church mission work or community service have to do with Sunday morning sermons?"

Others around the table nodded and looked at Micah expectantly. Deacon Ames continued.

"With the money we'd make from being nationally televised, we could feed all the homeless in the area we want, if that's what we choose to do. What's the real deal here? Are you not ready to run with the big dogs?"

Deacon Ames slammed his fist on the table.

"Well Standing Rock is! I've been a deacon here for twenty-one years, and this church has been in the shadows of other churches with the same caliber of members and with the same potential we have for too long. If we want to grow and bring people in and be the church to reckon with in Richmond, we need to seize this opportunity. If we don't, Mr. Carter will be knocking on a door across town."

Micah knew he was outnumbered. He sighed and tried again.

"I'll go home and pray about this again, everyone. But in my spirit, in my heart, I don't feel we should worry about growing the church's numbers and budget until we can say that we're teaching the twenty-five hundred members we have how to live their walk with God every day, that we're teaching them how to love their neighbors as themselves.

"If we move forward with the TV ministry, I might be led to preach sermons on prosperity for the next year," Micah said. "But if one Sunday I decided to focus on faith or on the consequences of sin, I need to know that I'm not violating some tenet of the contract that could leave us owing more money or being yanked from the air.

"By allowing ourselves to be told what the focus of our ministry should be, we're basically selling ourselves to a television plantation."

Deacon Ames loosened his tie and pressed his lips together. He looked at Jason, who was seated next to Micah.

"What do you think?"

Micah glanced at Jason, whom many in the church considered an up-and-coming hotshot. Jason's hazel eyes and curly hair often caused young girls and women alike to swoon. He used his physical assets to his advantage, more than Micah liked, to recruit ministry volunteers or solicit donations for special church events, but Standing Rock's deacon and trustee board had viewed him as a perfect complement to Micah when he had applied for the assistant pastorship right out of seminary.

"Between Micah and Jason, we'll have the most talked about preachers in town. Standing Rock will grow by leaps and bounds!" Deacon Ames had declared on the day the committee had voted to hire him.

Micah's steady leadership and spellbinding sermons had indeed helped the congregation grow. Jason's powerful prayers and innate charisma had also clicked with the masses. Standing Rock had grown by nearly a thousand members since Micah's tenure began.

He and Jason had remained more acquaintances and colleagues than friends, though.

Micah was happy to chill with his wife at Mister P's, their favorite jazz restaurant in Richmond's Jackson Ward community, while the still-single Jason spent much of his free time traveling to D.C. to frequent the theater and visit friends.

Tonight the preachers' lack of connectedness was obvious to everyone present.

Jason, who had been on staff for two years, squirmed in his seat. He looked at Micah and shrugged at Deacon Ames's question.

"I'm sorry, Pastor, but I don't see the problem. If we want to be a twenty-first-century church, we have to act like it."

Sighs of relief reverberated around the table. Had people been holding their breath? Micah couldn't believe it.

Deacon Ames seized the ammunition.

"There you have it, Pastor. It's twenty-two against one. If you don't like the progress we're making, maybe it's time for you to move on."

This time there were audible gasps.

An ultimatum?

Micah wanted to laugh one second and shake himself the next to make sure he wasn't dreaming.

Deacon Ames looked down the length of the table at Micah and continued.

"I think I speak for us all when I say if you can't do as we're asking, maybe this is no longer the place for you. There will always be death and destruction in these streets. That's what poor, hopeless people do to each other. All we can do is pray for them. But this is an opportunity to take our ministry nationwide, possibly even international. Don't get caught up in little old Richmond's problems when we could be ministering to people around the world."

Micah rubbed the palm of his hand across his head and sat back in his chair.

"Look, ladies and gentlemen, I don't have a problem taking Standing Rock to the masses," Micah said. "I do have a problem with rushing into this agreement without considering all the pros and cons.

"I know this is exciting. I know it could be a great opportunity. But I also know to trust my gut, that inner voice of God. And right now God is telling me that he will bless us without us having to pigeonhole our church into delivering only one kind of message."

The group sat stone-faced, refusing to meet Micah's eyes. Deacon Turner looked at his hands. Deaconess Pugh stared into the eyes of her husband, who sat across the table from her. Sister Grady flipped the pages of her Bible. Even Elvira Lewis, who was usually batting her eyes at Micah or smoothing a too-snug blouse over her ample bosom, fingered her copy of the contract from PGU without acknowledging Micah's comments.

Micah stood and straightened his tie.

"Since we don't seem to be of one accord tonight, it might be more productive if this meeting continues without me."

He looked toward Deacon Ames, whose eyes were still flashing from the challenge he had issued.

"I didn't know churches hired and fired their pastors on a whim," Micah said. "We're not a corporation, right? We operate under God's authority. I'll go home and pray for God to give me clarity on my concerns. I'm asking each of you to ask for wisdom on how we should move forward as a church."

Micah's heart ached. Their silence told him where they stood. Whatever it took, Standing Rock was going to be televised on PGU.

"See you all on Sunday. Have a blessed evening."

Micah neatly stacked the pages of the PGU contract he had been poring over and tucked them into his folder. He strolled out of the room and gently closed the door behind him. He stopped by his study to grab his gray suit jacket and headed out a side door to get to his car.

A passage of Scripture came to him as he drove out of the parking lot. He decided to use it as the text for Sunday's sermon—just in case it was his last.

15

"My goodies, my goodies, my goodies, not my goodies . . ."

R & B singer Ciara's hit song "Goodies" blasted from a room on the first floor. Charlotte strolled down the narrow hallway and knocked on the door of the room occupied by Shelly, a nineteen-year-old shelter resident.

"That's a decent theme song baby, but it's Bible study time," Charlotte yelled over the thumping beat. "Come on out and join us."

"No thanks!" the girl replied through the door as she lowered the volume on her CD player.

Charlotte strolled toward the shelter's family room, where Erika was waiting for her in the doorway. Charlotte didn't seem surprised to see her.

"Hey, Ms. Erika, come on in. We're about to start."

In her faded overalls, with those salt-and-pepper braids pulled back into a ponytail secured by a red rubber band at the nape of her neck, Charlotte was a sister-girl version of Mrs. Garrett, the boarding school headmistress on the 1980s sitcom *The Facts of Life*.

Charlotte grabbed Erika's hand and led her to a seat on a brown tweed sofa near where she would be sitting. She always positioned herself in the center of the room, facing two sofas and a hodgepodge of chairs she pulled from throughout the shelter.

"Is this cool?"

Erika was tempted to move to the rear of the room but didn't.

"Can you believe I made it to a Bible study?" she said and smiled, hoping Charlotte couldn't tell she had been crying.

"I can believe it," she said and patted Erika's hand. "I knew it was just a matter of time. Where else can you turn for abiding love?"

Love.

The very mention of that word made the tears well up in Erika's eyes again. She looked down at her hands.

The people she loved always seemed to hurt her: her mother, who had been too self-centered to sacrifice her romantic life and travels to focus on her child's needs, and Elliott, who had seemed to be the perfect boyfriend until he struck her for the first time because he thought she had looked at another man. That beating had led to an apology and then another beating, and years later, here she was.

Erika's stay in the shelter included a mandatory support group. She hadn't shared much during the sessions, but listening to the other women's stories and to the counselor's responses helped her realize that in enduring the beatings from Elliott, she had in some way been trying to punish herself for being so resentful toward and angry with her mother.

She realized that a part of her believed the horrible things one of her stepfathers had said about her. Even if people thought she was pretty, she was rotten inside. She had a loose mother, a father who had rarely called or paid child support, and nothing else going for her.

Maybe that's why her mother had never considered her worthy of sacrifices or attention. Maybe that's why Elliott had to beat her into shape.

She squeezed her eyes tight to block those thoughts.

Love? What makes it abiding?

I AM love.

The gentle voice that spoke to her heart startled her.

She looked up at Charlotte, who had been observing her. She saw compassion in the woman's eyes.

"I know," Charlotte said softly. "It will be all right."

Charlotte rose to greet Kathy and several other women who were coming from dinner. Volunteers from a Red Cross babysitting club came on Thursday nights to play with the children living in the shelter during the ninety-minute Bible study, so Kathy didn't have Xavier with her.

By the time Charlotte opened the session with a prayer, half the shelter's residents had claimed a seat.

Erika fidgeted on the sofa next to Kathy.

Why am I so nervous? Serena used to talk about God like he lived in our apartment. I know the other people here tonight. What's up with me?

Erika noticed that she was one of the few who didn't have a Bible with her. Charlotte passed her one and asked the women to turn to Matthew 9:19–22.

Tina, the forty-year-old wife of a Texas judge, stood and read the passage aloud.

"So Jesus arose and followed him, and so did His disciples. And suddenly, a woman who had a flow of blood for twelve years came from behind and touched the hem of His garment; for she said to herself, 'If only I may touch His garment, I shall be made well.' But Jesus turned around, and when He saw her He said, 'Be of good cheer, daughter; your faith has made you well.' And the woman was made well from that hour."

"Thank you, Tina," Charlotte said.

She continued. "Our theme tonight is 'Touched by His Love.' Those of you who come regularly know we don't do this in a sermon format, but I'd like to share a theme to give us a sense of what we can expect to take away from the study.

"All of you here this evening have been hurt by someone you love. Tonight we're looking at an example of real love in action.

"In the passage of Scripture Tina read, Jesus was going about his business, making his way through the crowd, when he felt something. It made him stop. Somehow he knew what he felt was from the hand of someone who desperately needed him.

"The beautiful thing about this incident is that Jesus took time to find out who she was and what she wanted. He could have decided he was too busy to be bothered. He could have ignored her touch. He could have been angry that someone had the nerve to put her hands on his clothes.

"But he met this woman with compassion. He showed her love. He showed her that she was worthy of love. Can anyone here relate to this?"

No one responded.

"Oh, come on. Someone share."

Mandy, a slender brunette whose two front teeth had been knocked out by her live-in boyfriend, stood in the back.

"It's hard to believe stories like this are true. Why would Jesus stop to help a stranger? My boyfriend used to say nothing in life is free. Whatever you get, you owe somebody for it."

Kamika, who sat on a love seat adjacent to Mandy, rolled her eyes.

"See, that's what landed most of us in this shelter—thinking we deserved to be mistreated or believing that abuse was a normal part of the romantic package. A relationship can't be all good, so we have to pay in some way, right? I'm glad I finally realized the price was too high."

Charlotte nodded.

"Both of you raise good points. But with God, Mandy, there are no strings attached. All he asks is that we come to him with a sincere heart. He knows all, and he knows our hearts. We could never pay enough or do enough to earn God's love. I gave my life to God twenty years ago, and I still mess up every day. But God loves me anyway, just like he loved the woman who dared to touch his garment. He didn't ask her what sins she had committed that day. He didn't ask her if she had joined a church or if she had any problems.

"He blessed her because she was sincere and, deep in her heart, longed to be near him. That's all he asks of us too. We can't physically touch Jesus's garments today, but when we open our hearts to him, he can touch our souls.

He speaks to us all the time. How many of you hear that gentle voice you sometimes think is your conscience or your sixth sense?"

Erika gingerly raised her hand but put it up higher when she looked around and saw others had theirs raised too.

Charlotte nodded.

"Don't ignore it. It's your internal compass. It's God telling you that he's touching you with his love."

She paused to see if anyone else wanted to comment.

Clara, a grandmother of five who last week had walked out on her husband of forty-three years, stood with tears streaming from her blue eyes. She removed her glasses and mopped her wrinkled face with her weathered hand.

"I've been walking with God for as long as I can remember, and I still found it hard to listen to him.

"When my pastor kept telling me to stay with my husband and try to please him, even after he broke my nose and treated me like a servant, that small voice you're talking about told me to love myself enough to leave. It told me that my children deserved better and that I would be covered by God's love no matter what."

Clara shook her head at the memories.

"In the week I've been in this depressing, cramped shelter, I've felt freer than I have in years. I have no money, I'm too old to work, and I can't go live with my kids because they've taken their father's side in this.

"But I know that God is looking out for me. If Jesus felt the needs of that woman who touched his garment, he knows I need him now too."

Everyone, including Erika, needed a tissue by the time Clara had taken her seat.

Erika thought about the baby she was carrying and her fear of becoming a mother. She wept for the family she longed to have—she, Elliott, and their child, living happily in their beautiful home, forever. Tonight she let that dream die.

She didn't want to wind up like Clara by returning to a prison made by a man who professed to love her. She didn't want to be elderly and alone with nowhere to go. She didn't want to raise her child in a home where the child learned to accept abuse, like she had, or to be abusive.

She grabbed a tissue from the box that had circulated to her from the other end of the room and dabbed at her eyes.

I AM love.

The voice didn't seem so strange to her anymore.

16

Serena swerved into the driveway and pulled inside the garage. She had asked Micah to meet her at the house by seven o'clock, giving her just enough time to grill a pair of steaks, microwave some sweet potatoes, and throw together some other side dishes. She had some exciting news to share.

Micah had sounded agitated when she called, but she had been too excited and distracted to ask him for details. He had promised to be home when she asked, though.

She pressed the button to lower the garage door and pulled off her winter white cashmere coat as she entered the kitchen. She draped it across the back of the wrought-iron chair stationed at the island before washing her hands in the sink.

She hummed an Alicia Keys melody as she scrubbed potatoes and chopped broccoli.

Maybe I should add some soft music to the mix, she thought. She opened a cabinet door off to the side of the kitchen and switched on the surround sound stereo system.

When Micah walked in forty-five minutes later, the candlelit kitchen smelled inviting. Serena had changed from the black pantsuit she had worn to work into tan pull-on stretch pants with a matching zip-up top. She had taken a quick shower, pinned her hair up in a chignon, and lightly sprayed on the perfume Micah loved. Anita Baker's latest groove was playing softly.

She sat at the table, sipping a glass of water and smiling broadly.

His eyes widened.

"What's all this?"

He took off his black quarter-length leather jacket and walked over for his welcome home greeting. The kiss was sweet and tender, as usual.

Serena evaded his question.

"What's all what? A wife can't make a nice, inviting meal for her man? Just enjoy," she said and smiled coyly. She could tell, though, that Micah was distracted.

"What is it?" she asked.

An unfamiliar sadness canvassed his face. He sighed.

"Long day. I'll tell you about it later. Don't keep me waiting. What's all this for?"

Serena ran her hand down his clean-shaven cheek. Just last week, ten days into the new year, he had shaved off the goatee he had grown during the holiday season. She missed the rugged look it had given him, but this wasn't bad.

She had planned to share her news after dinner, but she realized Micah wasn't up for the suspense. Hopefully, what she had to say would cheer him up.

She leaned across the round glass table, took his hands, and kissed them.

"God willing, you will be a father soon."

Micah looked at her stomach and then into her eyes. "Are you . . . ?"

She placed a single finger on his lips to silence him and struggled to stave off the pain that was still capable of piercing her heart.

"No, no, baby, I'm not pregnant," she began and felt a twinge of hurt at his crestfallen expression.

"But there is good news. My appointment with Dr. Knott and with the in vitro specialist, Dr. Ritter, went well today. They said they were sorry you had a last-minute emergency and couldn't make it, but here's the news:

"Dr. Ritter said we can come in as early as next week and implant up to four eggs. They'll watch closely to make sure there are no more ectopic pregnancies, but they're confident that this is the best way to overcome the infertility. And here's even better news: my insurance will cover 50 percent of the bill!"

Micah smiled and kissed her, but she had expected more. She pulled away and looked into his eyes.

"Aren't you excited? Isn't this what we both wanted? To have a baby?"

Her stomach fluttered.

Be with me, Lord.

Micah kissed her lips.

"I love you, and you know I want you to have my babies. But I have some news too, and it's not the best.

"Standing Rock members held a meeting last night and asked the congregation to vote me out as pastor. They're allowing me to preach until they can rally more support and an official vote is taken. I've heard they want Jason Lyons to step in as interim pastor."

Micah stood, plunged his hands in his pockets, and turned away from his wife. He expelled a bitter laugh.

"I'm guessing I'll be voted out as pastor and Jason will be given the job in a few weeks, just in time for the church to prepare for a spring premiere of the Sunday services on the PGU Gospel Network."

Serena lost it.

"They held a meeting and you weren't aware of it? They're trying to fire you because you didn't want to go on TV? Do we serve the same God?"

She rose from her seat and paced back and forth in front of the table.

"Standing Rock members will never go for this. They love you, Micah. They know you're anointed by God. When you preach on Sunday, tell them why you don't want to rush into the contract with PGU. God will give you favor."

She walked over to Micah, whose back was still turned to her, and hugged him.

He lowered his head and said in a barely audible voice, "I don't know, love. This is serious. They're trying to convince the members that I'm standing in the way of twenty-first-century progress. They're spreading the word that I've lost my touch."

Serena was about to launch into another tirade, when it struck her. She circled around her husband until she faced him.

"What does this mean for next week's surgery?"

Micah pulled her close so that she was forced to rest her head on his shoulder. She knew whatever he was going to say, he didn't want her to see the pain in his eyes.

"Serena, from what I hear, if I'm fired soon, they're not

planning to give me a severance package. Part of the twenty thousand dollars we've saved for the in vitro process may have to be used to pay our bills."

Her hands fell from around Micah's waist, and she backed away from him. The steamer pinged, indicating the broccoli was ready. The oven timer went off, signaling that the yeast rolls were too.

Her throat tightened.

She glared at Micah. "Everything is ready on time, except when it comes to me having a baby. It's not the right season. It's not my time. Is that what I'm going to hear again?"

Serena slid to the floor and doubled over with sobs. She was so tired. She just wanted a baby. Her baby.

She thought about the last email she had received from Erika three months ago, informing her that Erika was pregnant. Living in a shelter. Estranged from her abusive husband. And pregnant. What good timing.

"Why can't you give me this one thing, God? Haven't I been faithful? What more do you want from me?"

I want all of you.

"I don't have anything else to give!" she yelled.

Serena swiped at her tears. She had been in this place with God before. As angry as she was, this time she refused to push God away. She needed him to help her through this pain.

Micah approached her as she sat on the floor, leaning against the cabinets just below the sink. When he stopped abruptly and turned his back to her, his heaving shoulders told her she wasn't the only one hurting.

Right now, though, they couldn't comfort each other. They needed someone strong enough for the both of them.

17

The phone had been ringing nonstop since Tuesday as word spread of Micah's precarious position with Standing Rock. His voice mail at the church filled up each time he emptied it.

"Pastor, this is Sister Grady," she had said before pausing dramatically. "I don't know what to say, except that I'm praying that God's will be done in this situation. Whatever happens, Sister Grady loves you."

"Yo, Pastor, dis here is Little Tim," said the fifty-year-old choir member who bore a striking resemblance to rapper Jay-Z and had joined Standing Rock a year ago with his new wife and stepdaughter. Micah had counseled Tim and Carla several times about the issues blended families often faced.

"Hey, man," Tim continued, "I was at dat church meeting they held on Thursday night about the situation with the television network and your fights with the church leaders over the contract. Personally, I think we should take all the exposure that's offered to us, man. But I respect you and know you probably have your reasons for being against it.

You ain't a bad-looking brother, so you could shine on TV, you know? I'm just giving a brother a call, 'cause I don't want to see you go, man. I'm praying for you and hope you'll think about it. Peace out."

Micah had laughed heartily after listening to the message.

Some folks hear the word TV *and lose their minds*, he mused.

"If I had a problem with someone wanting to write a *book* about the church, I bet half these people wouldn't give a flip," he muttered before deleting Tim's message and listening to the fifteenth one in the mailbox.

"Rev. McDaniels, you know they trying to fire you! Watch your back. You're a good man, but sometimes you gotta fight fire with fire! Give 'em heck, Pastor!"

The caller had hung up without leaving her name, but Micah had recognized Hazel Timm's gravelly, nasal voice. Years of smoking had made her sound more male than female, but people had grown accustomed to it.

Micah was heartened to know that she was rooting for him, even if she was doing so anonymously.

Jason Lyons had left Micah what was supposed to sound like an apologetic message.

"Hey, Micah, I'm just calling to say I'm not happy about how any of this is going down. I'm just trying not to make waves, man. You're a good brother, so whatever happens you're going to be okay. Hang in there, man."

Micah shook his head in disgust.

"God forgive me for what I'm thinking right now," he said angrily before deleting the voice mail.

He listened to an hour's worth of messages before deciding he'd had enough.

I'm trying to gauge the sentiment of the congregation by these calls, he realized. *I need to focus on what God wants me to do.*

"If I'm wrong, please reveal it to me," he prayed aloud. "I know that pride goes before a fall. I know that even your sons in the ministry can get it wrong sometimes. Let me know if I'm wrong, Lord."

His eyes flew open when he heard the soft click of the door closing. His wife stood there, gazing at him.

Serena's eyes were bloodshot from crying. She walked over to the cushioned chair across from Micah's desk and plopped herself in it. "I tried all day to call and cancel the in vitro appointment, but I couldn't. I finally decided to come check on you. I just eavesdropped on your prayer.

"You aren't wrong, babe," she said softly. "I admit, I don't fully understand why you don't want to travel this path. TV ministries have been a blessing for a lot of churches and for the people who watch. Those broadcasts have helped save souls or bolstered some people's faith. Even when I was mad at God years ago, I found myself drawn to the stations with inspirational programming.

"All I know is that when God told you to give up a promising medical career, you obeyed and he blessed you. When you were in a waiting season and had to toil at the post office until he blessed you with this congregation, it was difficult. But you waited for God to tell you to move instead of taking the first offer that came along to pastor a church.

"And now here you are again, making a decision no one understands, maybe not even you. But as you've told me since the day I met you, Micah, you have to listen to what God is speaking to your heart. If you do what these church leaders and the congregation want and it isn't what God

119

has in mind, then you're outside his will. You won't be blessed, and Standing Rock won't be blessed."

Micah got up from his desk and walked over to hug Serena.

"Are you preaching to me, Mrs. McDaniels?"

She smiled wryly.

"Do you need a word, Pastor? Let's go home."

It was just two o'clock, but Micah didn't protest.

They left the office hand in hand. Serena pulled her Audi behind Micah's Jeep and followed at his leisurely pace. He was either thinking really hard or praying, Serena surmised, because her odometer barely registered the speed limit.

On the forty-minute drive home, Serena listened to the CeCe Winans CD that had always soothed her when she needed to be reminded of God's love. The lyrics to the songs on *Alone in His Presence* were a meditation to her spirit.

"I'm safe and sound, serene and calm, whenever I'm here, I know you're with me," CeCe sang.

The words gave Serena peace. This morning the troubles with Micah had been made more difficult when she had opened a new email from Erika, who shared that she was planning to enroll in childbirth preparation classes soon.

Serena felt guilty for being jealous of her sweet and troubled friend.

I know you're going to see us through this, God, Serena prayed silently as she drove. *Somehow, some way.*

18

As daylight peeked through the flimsy blinds covering the bedroom window, Erika opened her eyes and listened for the wailing.

Jose, an infant living two doors down the hall with his mother, Juanita, had been awake throughout the night, interrupting sleep for everyone in the shelter with his piercing cry. Erika had heard Juanita pacing the hall with him in her arms, singing lullabies in Spanish. Now, finally, there was silence. The infant gas drops the shelter's night shift manager had gone out and purchased must have worked.

"I'm worn out," Erika sighed.

She turned her body away from the door, briefly lay on her back, then rolled onto her right side. At six months pregnant, she was finally beginning to show. Since she was usually paper thin, the moderate protrusion in her belly made her appear bloated to others, but she felt like a Pillsbury dough girl.

Erika had always envisioned a blissful first pregnancy. She and Elliott would work together to decorate a nursery on the second floor of their home. They would toss potential names back and forth and decide on one they both loved. Elliott would attend childbirth classes with her, help deliver their baby, and never see the need to abuse her again.

Certainly that last part had been a fantasy. Her weekly counseling sessions with a psychologist who recently began volunteering at the shelter had helped her realize how much power she had given to Elliott, how he had beaten her not only physically but also emotionally. It made sense that after a while she had given Pavlov-like responses, doing what she needed to do to keep the peace.

Erika repositioned her lumpy pillow on the twin bed and closed her eyes, willing herself into five more minutes of sleep. Just as she was beginning to drift off, Kathy's feet hit the wooden floor.

"Whew!" she said and raised her arms above her head for a good stretch. She ran her fingers through her short bobbed hairstyle, massaged her temples, and continued to talk.

"That darn baby! I have to go to a job-training session today, and I didn't get any sleep with all that crying Jose did last night."

She looked over at Xavier sleeping peacefully in his crib.

"At least *you* let Mommy rest."

Erika, with her eyes still closed and her head still resting on her pillow, nodded to acknowledge that she heard Kathy, who continued chattering, as she did every morning.

Hasn't she figured out yet that I'm not a morning person? I need a cup of decaf coffee and at least an hour with very little stimulation to get myself together.

"It's going to be a long day," Kathy continued. "I also have a counseling session with the Rev. Ms. Charlotte."

"Oh?" Erika couldn't resist responding.

"Let her tell it, God will fix everything that's wrong," Kathy sneered. "I've been to those Bible studies. But where was God when my husband was punching out my teeth? Where was the man upstairs when I spent years praying for my husband to turn back into the kind and generous person he was before we got married?"

Erika opened her eyes and saw the scowl on Kathy's face. Her roommate's eyes held sorrow.

She understood Kathy's pain, but she had no answers. She had asked similar questions about Elliott in recent months.

She sat up and swung her feet over the side of the bed and slipped on the worn pink slippers she had fished from the shelter's closet of donated clothes. She hated the color pink and despised the fact that although the slippers were clean, the material was matted. But her feet were always cold on the shelter's wood floors, and she needed something other than just her socks to keep her warm.

She shrugged at Kathy's comments.

"Charlotte is nice. I talk to her about the things I've been through, and she's not shocked. She's been through a lot herself. Her faith is part of her."

Kathy rolled her eyes and flopped across her bed. Erika watched her, waiting to see if the discussion would continue. She hated to see Kathy hold the same disdain she had held for God until recently. If there wasn't a God, she wasn't sure who was keeping her sane as she contemplated her future with a baby, no income, and no permanent place to live.

"She can save the Lord for her next client sleeping in this bed," Kathy said.

Xavier stirred in his crib but didn't open his eyes. Kathy unfurled her long, dancer's legs and took two steps to where he lay. Erika watched her gazing at the rhythmic pattern of her son's breathing as he sucked his thumb and clutched the crib sheet with his other hand.

Kathy's smile faded as she walked away from the baby over to the mirror hanging on the back of the bedroom door. She peered at her café-au-lait complexion and touched the dark circles under each eye.

"I used to be so beautiful," she said softly as tears pooled in her eyes.

Erika walked over to her and placed a hand on her shoulder.

"You still are, Kathy," she said, looking at the woman through the mirror. "Your husband was wrong."

Kathy smiled at Erika and turned to face her and change the subject.

"Enough drama. What are you up to today?"

Erika was relieved to move on to something else.

"Since I've helped so many women leaving the shelter decorate their apartments with Goodwill finds, Charlotte's taking me to meet a professional interior designer. And this evening she's going with me to childbirth classes. She's been so wonderful."

Kathy crossed the small room and picked up Xavier, who had finally awakened and was reaching for her.

"Tell Charlotte I can postpone our meeting if she needs to."

She left the room with the baby and closed the door behind her.

Erika stood there, wondering if Kathy was going to stay angry and defensive. Her own guard was still up, but slowly and surely she was beginning to believe she could go on and thrive.

Today would put her one step closer.

19

A fter you, Ms. Wilson."
Charlotte held the door for Erika and followed her
into the corporate office and showroom of D. Haven Interior Designs.

The cozy northern Virginia showroom was bathed in
mellow lighting that drew attention to the elegant pieces
of strategically placed furniture. In a corner off to the right,
brighter lighting over a glass-topped table with an intri-
cately designed base provided a space where clients could
sit and look through color and fabric swatches.

Awards lined the shelves behind the customer service
counter from which a receptionist rose and offered Erika
and Charlotte glasses of wine. Both women declined.

"Even if you weren't pregnant, you'd need to be clear
headed for this meeting," Charlotte said. "D. Haven is one
of the best in the business. Get this brother to hire you,
and you're on your way."

In recent months Charlotte had been trying to help Erika
define what she'd like to do as a career. Erika's newfound
interest in decorating had led her to rearrange the furniture

in the shelter's family room and to sew curtains with material someone had donated to Naomi's Nest years ago.

"You can take your real estate licensing exam again and try to resume that career, but it's going to take a lot of networking, getting out there and making contacts and selling your business," Charlotte had said.

Erika had nixed the idea.

"The thrill is gone for chasing the sale. What else can I do?"

Charlotte had peered at her over the top of her red-rimmed reading glasses.

"What else do you want to do? What else do you have an interest in? You've decorated rooms here at the shelter. You've helped Doris, Becky, and some of the other women find the perfect items to reflect their tastes and create ambience in the apartments they now call home. Your whole countenance changes when you're working with interior decorating. I've watched you. Why not start there?"

Two phone calls and two days later, Erika and Charlotte were in the Fairfax County studio of D. Haven Interior Designs to meet the senior designer, Gabrielle Donovan.

Gabrielle leaned against the doorway of her office on the far side of the design studio and watched as Charlotte and Erika approached her. She was petite but not quite as short as Erika and had the most beautiful hair Erika had ever seen, flowing in waves past her shoulders. Her handshake left Erika wondering if the woman was a female bodybuilder.

"Erika, so nice to meet you. I understand you're interested in interior design?"

127

Erika smiled and tried not to wince when Gabrielle finally released her hand.

"Nice to meet you as well, Gabrielle. Yes, I'm interested in interior decorating. Thank you for taking time to meet with me."

An odd look crossed Gabrielle's face. She entered her office and beckoned for Erika and Charlotte to follow her.

When the women were seated, she leaned across her desk and gave Erika a condescending smile.

"Erika, I enjoy meeting with people serious about this field. Charlotte told me when she and I spoke a couple of days ago that you have been a real estate agent and have a bachelor's degree in marketing. That provides a promising foundation for moving to this kind of work.

"What I need to know from you, however, is what you want to accomplish. A few moments ago, you indicated an interest in interior decorating. Interior decorators and interior designers are not one and the same. If you want be a decorator, you can leave here this afternoon, get a local printer to design you some business cards, and have some clients by tomorrow.

"If you're interested in interior design, you must study in an accredited program for two to four years, get solid experience in a reputable interior design firm, have some undergraduate architectural courses under your belt, and eventually be licensed to work in this industry.

"This process is not for the faint of heart or for anyone who wants to dabble in decorating. It can take you anywhere from two to six years, depending on all of the factors I've shared, but in the end, you'll have the skills, ability, and credibility to take your career as far as you'd like.

"If you're interested in design, you're in the right place. Mr. Haven does excellent work and is an excellent mentor and boss. He's well respected in the industry and has the name recognition to snag us commercial and residential clients, as well as opportunities that might otherwise be difficult to secure.

"If you're still interested, we can pair you with a staff designer for a day or two and have him or her give you some tips on how to choose complementary color swatches, fabrics for sofas, et cetera."

Gabrielle clasped her hands together and sat back in her chair. She looked expectantly at Erika.

Erika smiled at the self-assured woman. She could tell that Gabrielle was familiar with her background. The condescending tone said it all. But as Gabrielle had laid all the pros and cons on the table, Erika had made a decision.

She was at the point in her life where the choices she made could determine how far she'd go for the rest of her life. She could sit here today and choose an easier path that offered stability and a satisfying career as an interior decorator, or she could challenge herself to do what was necessary to develop what sounded like a rewarding and exciting career in an industry in which she could thrive beyond her expectations.

With a baby on the way and the need to support herself, Erika decided that today was the time to step out on that faith Charlotte was always talking about. Her heart was telling her not to settle anymore.

She had settled with Elliott, whom she had considered a prize despite his flaws. She had done it when she stayed for four years in a marriage that left her feeling worthless.

Today she was going to make a good choice for herself, by herself. As she prepared to answer Gabrielle, an excitement and peace filled her.

This is your season, my child.

That small, still voice didn't leave Erika unsettled anymore. She recognized her friend and Father now and wondered what had taken her so long to hear him.

Erika looked Gabrielle in the eyes.

"Interior design seems to be a better fit for where I'd like to go in my career. Yes, my undergrad degree is in marketing, which was valuable during the five years I worked as a real estate agent. I even took an architectural design course in college."

Gabrielle's eyes brightened.

"That training was wonderful in helping me sell clients on a property, because I could help them visualize how to put their own stamp on a particular space.

"I'd love to spend a few hours shadowing you each week, Gabrielle, or maybe helping answer phones. Whatever I can do to be in this environment learning the business, I would be delighted."

Gabrielle's countenance had changed.

"Erika, we'd be delighted to help you. Mr. Haven isn't here to meet you today because he had a previously scheduled meeting, but he told me to follow my instincts in what kind of assistance or guidance to share with you.

"Since he's given me that authority, how about I offer you something better than a volunteer or administrative position? Want to be the company's intern? You can shadow me on interviews with clients, accompany me to showrooms, and help me sift through fabrics and other items to find the perfect pieces for a particular project. Are you interested?"

Wide-eyed and speechless, Erika looked at Charlotte.

Charlotte smiled. Erika could tell she was trying to mask her excitement and remain professional.

"Obviously, Gabrielle, Erika sees this as a wonderful opportunity. When could she start?"

Gabrielle shrugged, but before she could reply, Erika interrupted.

"There's just one thing I think you should be aware of, since you're extending such a wonderful opportunity," Erika said. "I'm six months pregnant and living in a battered women's shelter in D.C. I have no family support system or place to call my own."

Gabrielle nodded.

"I was informed about all of that yesterday, Erika. I know you're in a tough situation. If you want to try to do this, we're willing to work around your schedule and allow you to come in when you can.

"I'll be honest—it's going to be hard at first trying to juggle baby care with the demands and deadlines of this job, but if you want to pursue this, I'm here to help. Mr. Haven has a heart for people struggling to make it, so he's on board too."

Erika smiled and then looked down at her hand, which was bare of the elegant ring she had once been so proud of. Shame coursed through her as she realized that Gabrielle was familiar with her circumstances. In a split second, she made a decision. She was no longer going to be afraid of people finding out her truths or ashamed of her past.

Erika raised her head and looked Gabrielle in the eyes.

"Please tell Mr. Haven I said thank you and I hope to meet him soon," she said. "I'm looking forward to being your intern. When can I start?"

Gabrielle threw back her head and laughed.

"A woman after my own heart—doesn't like to waste time. How about tomorrow? Can you come in for two hours? Since you're getting farther along in your pregnancy, I don't want to overload you. Let's start there, and we'll see how things go."

She stood up and walked around the desk and leaned on it.

"This isn't going to be a piece of cake, Erika, but if you're willing to make sacrifices and work hard, it will all pay off."

As Gabrielle escorted her and Charlotte to the door, doubts dampened Erika's excitement. How was she going to get the proper training with a baby? How was she going to pay for school, find time to study, and care for her child?

Charlotte placed her arm around Erika's shoulders and gave her a hug as they walked toward the van.

"Didn't I tell you she was something else?" Charlotte asked. "Mr. Haven used to serve on our board, and he's brought Gabrielle to a couple of fund-raising functions.

"Don't you go fretting about the obstacles you're facing for this position, Erika. Gabrielle didn't have to offer you an internship, especially with you being six months pregnant. She saw your promise. She wanted to hire you."

They stopped in front of the van, and Charlotte unlocked Erika's door. She helped Erika climb into the seat and walked around to the driver's side.

When she settled into the driver's seat and started the van, Erika was staring out the window.

"What is it, Erika?"

"This is a great opportunity," Erika said, her voice quivering. "I know I can do this job well. What I'm questioning is whether I can be a good mother. Add a high-powered career to my lack of parenting skills, and I might be in over my head."

20

Micah opened the massive front door to his home and froze.

"Pops?"

He stared at his father, who was a mirror image of Micah with his deep chocolate complexion, chiseled jawline, and handsome smile. If the graying temples didn't give Avery McDaniels away, the two could have passed for brothers.

"You flew here? By yourself? From Oklahoma?"

Mr. McDaniels grabbed his son and gave him a bear hug.

He laughed and said, "Can I come in, son?"

Micah stepped aside and let his father enter. He retrieved the suitcase from the brick porch and set it inside the foyer. When he closed the door and turned to his father, the two men locked eyes.

"I never understood why you gave up a promising medical career for the ministry, but I know you're a good man, Micah. Your mama told me what these church folk are trying to do to you. I know if you've decided to fight them, you have good reasons. I had to come and let you know I'm here for you. I'm proud of you, son."

The two men embraced again, and Micah struggled to keep his tears at bay. If anything could fuel them, though, it would be the presence of his father.

"I'm so glad you came, Pops," Micah said. "Flying wasn't so bad, was it?"

Mr. McDaniels cracked a wry smile.

"Yeah, yeah, yeah," he said and walked toward the family room to take a seat. "I guess it beats driving nineteen hours to get here. Where's my daughter-in-law?"

"She's in our bedroom; let me get her."

Micah climbed the stairs two at a time. He found Serena standing in her closet trying to figure out what to wear to work the next day. He tiptoed behind her and grabbed her around the waist.

She turned toward him and put her arms around his neck.

"I haven't seen that handsome smile lately. What's up?"

"Guess who flew into town?"

"Is your mom downstairs?"

"Nope. Pops is."

Serena stepped back and looked at him.

"Your father flew here? On an airplane? Check the driveway. You sure he didn't drive?"

Micah shrugged.

"A taxi dropped him off at the front door. He flew in on Aviator Airlines, according to the tag on his luggage. Come on."

Micah took Serena by the hand and led her down-stairs.

Mr. McDaniels greeted her with a big smile, a hug, and a kiss on the cheek.

"How's my girl doing? You look beautiful as always, Serena."

"Even in my sweats? Thanks, Pops. It's so good to see you! What on earth led you to break your vow and hop on a plane?"

As soon as she had asked the question, she knew. Micah had called last month and told his parents his job was in jeopardy.

As always, his mother had been unruffled.

She had told him, "It doesn't have to make sense to anybody why you have concerns about a TV ministry, baby. You just keep listening to the Lord. You just do what he tells you. In time it will make sense, as long as you honor what he says and don't worry about pleasing anybody else."

Mr. McDaniels had only grunted and said, "I'm praying for you, son."

Obviously, though, the conversation had shaken him. In the nearly eight years Micah had lived in Richmond, this was the first time he had flown. Micah's mom had sometimes visited by herself because of her husband's re-fusal to deal with what he considered the uncertainty and instability of airline travel.

Since becoming his daughter-in-law, Serena had tried to convince Mr. McDaniels to at least try Aviator Airlines. After all, she had handled a successful marketing campaign for the company during her advertising executive days.

The slogans, commercials, and magazine ads she developed were still being used by the airline.

"I'm proud of you, Pops," she said, beaming at her father-in-law. "Want something to eat or drink? I know they don't feed you much in the air these days."

Mr. McDaniels nodded. "That'd be nice. What do you have?"

The three of them strolled into the kitchen, with Serena on a mission to explore the refrigerator and Micah lingering back with his father.

"How long are you staying?" she asked when she emerged from the fridge with a two-liter of raspberry ginger ale, a bag of mixed salad greens, and a container of spaghetti left over from yesterday.

Mr. McDaniels settled at the table in the breakfast nook and sipped his soda as Serena heated the food.

"Just two days." He looked at Micah. "I wanted to set eyes on my boy myself and see how he was holding up. How are you, son?"

Micah shrugged and cast his eyes downward.

"I'm tough."

"I know you are." Mr. McDaniels winked at Serena.

She wondered if her fears were obvious.

He glanced at his Rolex.

"How about we catch up over a late afternoon game of golf?"

Micah grinned.

"You improved that swing yet, Pops? If not, I don't want to take you out there and pummel you, man."

Mr. McDaniels bared all of his teeth when he released a hearty laugh.

"Go get your clubs."

Serena smiled to herself as she set plates of food before both of them. She excused herself and left them engaging in a lighthearted banter.

In the shower upstairs, she uttered a prayer of thanks for this fellowship.

Lord, you know I love my husband, but living with him these past months has been trying. Thank you for the surprise visit from Pops. Let this be a special time for both of them.

Serena decided to leave them alone together as much as possible during Pops's short stay.

The bathroom mirror was fogged over by the time she emerged from her leisurely shower. She wiped her side with a cloth and smiled at her reflection.

It was just February, but Father's Day was being celebrated early in the McDaniels household. Melvin Gates had called that morning and asked to stop by. Serena was expecting him soon.

She went downstairs an hour later and found Micah and his father gone. A note on the refrigerator indicated that they had indeed gone out to take in a few rounds of golf.

"Hmph," she said to herself.and chuckled. "Guess I won't see them until nightfall."

She tidied up the kitchen and was surprised when the doorbell rang promptly at three o'clock. Her guest was right on time.

She smoothed the wrinkles forming on the front of her navy leisure suit and strode to the front door.

Melvin Gates was there with a bouquet of flowers.

"Hi. What are these for?" She took the pink roses from

her father and buried her nose in them, inhaling the sweet scent.

Melvin smiled and shrugged out of his coat as he followed her into the kitchen. Serena discarded the tissue paper that had covered the flower stems and filled a tall, wide-lipped crystal vase with tepid water. She positioned it in the center of the island that anchored the kitchen.

"Nice. Very nice. Thank you, Melvin."

"Just something I wanted to do," he said and took a seat at the breakfast table.

"I guess you heard," Serena said as she slid into the cushioned chair across from him. Sunlight streamed in through the partially opened blinds, making Melvin's deep brown eyes appear lighter than they were. In looking at him, Serena could see why her mother had been attracted to him.

Even now, in his late sixties, his medium brown complexion, shiny bald head, goatee, and perfect white teeth were magnetic. He exuded a confidence and a quietness that made him intriguing. Serena hadn't given it much thought before, but this afternoon she wondered if her mother had been one of many conquests.

She shook those thoughts from her head and returned to the present. Melvin was surveying her face intently.

She could tell he hadn't come with an agenda. He seemed to be really concerned about her.

"News travels fast in Richmond, even across the river. I know this is hard on Micah, but how are you doing?"

She lowered her eyes.

The tears began falling before she could suppress them.

Embarrassed for Melvin to see her crumbling, she turned away from the table but couldn't stop the waterfall.

"What is it, Serena? I know you and I don't have the closest of father-daughter relationships, but I want to help. If all I can do is pray with you, let me do that. Let me in."

Serena composed herself and walked into the family room. She sat on the edge of the sofa, her back still toward the kitchen. She wiped her eyes on her sleeve and tried to stop sniffling.

Melvin followed her and sat next to her, waiting.

"I'm okay, Melvin," she said softly once she had regained composure. "This is just so stressful. I can't believe they're treating Micah like this. He's a good man. God placed him at Standing Rock for a reason, and all because of an opportunity for a little TV exposure, they're turning on him. What kind of people do that?"

Melvin chuckled.

"Watch it, now," he said gently. "You're talking to an expert hypocrite here. I know all about how you can justify something when what you want to do feels right or glitters like gold."

Serena remained silent. She and Melvin had never discussed how he had come to have an affair with her mother when they served on a church committee together. She wasn't sure she wanted to know now.

Melvin sensed her trepidation.

"We can talk about me later, though. Just remind yourself of what you already know, Serena. People who come to church aren't perfect. They're hurt, lost, angry, jealous, and in need of spiritual healing. Unlike a trip to the emergency room, where you can get a prescription for painkillers or

140

antibiotics that will help you feel better or even cure you in a short amount of time, a commitment to God's church means you'll endure long-term, intensive work on the same issues, with the same people, for years.

"People don't spiritually mature at the same pace," he said. "Some of those church folks over there with dollar signs and dreams of stardom may not be at the level you are. You just have to pray and leave it to God to work on them."

Serena clutched a sofa pillow and tried to control her frustration.

"And in the meantime Micah will just be pushed out and have his reputation damaged," she said.

"Even if that happens, Serena, God knows his heart. God won't forsake him."

Serena took a deep breath.

"You're right, Melvin, you really are. I know God is in the middle of this, even when we think he's not. I guess I still have a lot of maturing to do myself. I've been longing for a baby, and this crisis at the church is one more obstacle. I guess I'm worried about Micah, but I'm selfishly worried about the disruption in my own plans too."

"Don't beat yourself up about it, Serena. We're all selfish in some ways," Melvin said. "Nobody has it just right except Jesus, and even he asked to be spared the fate of death on the cross if he could be."

Serena wiped her eyes and smiled. Melvin had helped her?

She turned to face him.

"Melvin . . . thank you."

He opened his arms with a question in his eyes.

Serena smiled and moved closer.

For the first time since finding out he was her biological father, she embraced him. The way he clung to her let her know he had been dreaming of this moment for a long time.

Serena smiled through her tears. She cried for the years they had missed and for the anger and shame. She cried because when no one else could be here for her, the man she had never thought she would connect with was.

If God could bring this to pass, anything was possible.

21

Erika trudged down the stairs and paused near the plant stand on the landing to clutch her basketball-sized belly and catch her breath.

"I'm huffing and puffing like a track star, but I look like Fat Albert," she said aloud.

She was determined to make it to Bible study tonight, though. She had promised Charlotte she would come. After Charlotte had agreed to serve as her birthing partner, she would do anything the older woman asked, even if it meant tackling the staircase she dreaded these days.

Thank God tonight would be the last time she would have to do so. Shelly had agreed to give Erika her first-floor bedroom and move upstairs with Kathy and little Xavier. Erika chuckled at the thought. That was going to be interesting. Between Xavier and Shelly, Kathy would have two children on her hands, a fifteen-month-old and a nineteen-year-old.

Erika shuffled toward the shelter's family room and frowned when she realized the room was dark.

I can't believe Charlotte hasn't already arranged the room for Bible study, she thought. She glanced at her watch. It was 6:55 p.m. "Wonder if the location changed," she said softly.

She turned toward the hallway and prepared to make her way to the cozy nook just off the kitchen in case Charlotte had moved the meeting there. Before she could move, she heard a noise.

"Surprise!"

Erika's eyes widened, and she grasped her protruding belly. She squinted when the lights in the family room suddenly came on.

The shelter's twenty residents and five employees stood before her, beaming. Most of them held gifts wrapped in baby-themed paper.

The crowd parted so Charlotte, in the rear of the room, could step forward. She approached Erika with open arms and enveloped her in a hug.

"We hoped this wouldn't send you into labor, but we wanted to surprise you with a shower to help you get ready for the baby."

Charlotte kissed Erika on the cheek and laughed at her stunned expression. Erika's eyes filled with tears when Kathy, Mandy, and Shelly surrounded her in a group hug.

"You betta stop cryin', girl," Doris said. "That there baby is going to do enough of that soon."

Laughter filled the room. Erika couldn't help chuckling herself.

Kathy, holding Xavier in one arm, grabbed Erika's hand and led her to the middle of the room to a tweed-covered chair decorated with blue streamers and blue and white ribbons.

"Sit here, madame," she said and made a sweeping gesture.

Erika laughed and sank into the chair. She wiped her moist eyes with the back of her hand.

"You guys are something else. Why did you go to all this trouble?"

"What trouble?"

The owner of the familiar voice stood behind the chair and covered Erika's eyes.

Startled, she turned and was greeted by Becky's smile.

"What are you doing here? You're not moving back in, are you?"

Laughter erupted again.

"No repeat customers!" Charlotte answered from across the room. "We allow you guys to come back and visit. That's the only way we want Naomi's Nest alumni to return—for visits or to volunteer."

Becky nodded at Charlotte and sat in the chair next to Erika's.

"I heard you were expecting and wanted to come tonight to celebrate with you. The baby is going to be beautiful, because you are. I'm still loving my apartment. Thanks for coming out and helping me decorate it."

Erika hugged Becky's neck tightly.

"Okay, everyone," Charlotte said. "Since we opted to have a shower instead of Bible study tonight, let's open up with a prayer before we move on to the silly baby games and some other fun at Ms. Erika's expense."

After the opening prayer, as the group prepared to play

"Name That Baby Item" and "Best Advice for the New Mom," Charlotte announced the arrival of two special guests.

"Erika hasn't met one of them, and the other one has known her only a short time, but she's committed to serving them both and becoming as savvy in her new career as they already are."

Gabrielle sauntered into the family room with a grin as big as her native Texas. Her arm was linked through a handsome gentleman's.

"Everyone, this is Gabrielle Donovan and Derrick Haven. Mr. Haven owns the interior design studio where Erika has interned for six weeks," Charlotte said. "He flew in from Paris tonight and insisted on stopping by."

Derrick didn't hear the introduction; his eyes were glued to Erika's face. She hadn't heard for the same reason.

"Hey, you," he said and smiled before extending his hand. "Remember me?"

Erika tried to ignore her racing pulse and grasped his hand.

I am a pregnant, married woman who is estranged from her husband and living in a shelter for battered women. What's gotten into me?

She ignored her thoughts and tried to mask her shock with a smile and small talk.

"Yes, I remember you. The guy at Goodwill. So you're my boss? You're D. Haven?"

He laughed and pulled up a chair next to her.

"It's a small world. I wasn't sure it was you, but when Charlotte called the office and asked me about helping a woman named Erika, I remembered our meeting that day

146

at the store and how you were helping your friends select just the right items for their places. I could tell then that you had a good eye for detail and that you were in tune with the tastes and personalities of your 'clients.'"

Erika was still stunned.

"What were you doing in Goodwill? Do you work there? It's a long way from the posh office setup you have in Fairfax County."

Derrick shrugged.

"I'm blessed to be a blessing. I volunteer in that store about once a month, sometimes at the register and sometimes helping sort donations. I wish I could do it more often, but as you probably know now that you work in my office, my schedule is off the charts."

Erika looked at him. His thick black eyebrows perfectly framed his smooth caramel face. He was as big as a linebacker but as laid-back as a playful puppy.

She wanted to ask him why he valued spending time at Goodwill instead of simply stroking a check or hosting a fund-raiser. Now was not the time or place, though.

Instead, she deadpanned, "Are you by any chance related to a man named Micah?"

"Excuse me?"

Erika shook her head, smiled, and hooked her thumbs into the straps of her blue-jean overalls. Finding another man as sincere and good as Serena's husband would probably be too good to be true.

"Never mind," she said and changed the subject. "I can't believe you came to my baby shower, that's all. Thank you."

"It's my pleasure, Erika," Derrick said sincerely. "I've

been hearing from Gabrielle and others on staff about how professional you are and how hard you work even with being pregnant.

"It's the right attitude to have in this business. You have to do excellent work, be courteous, and follow through on your word even when it's inconvenient.

"Gabrielle has shown me some of the rooms you've put together and some of the color palettes you've suggested after accompanying her to meetings with prospective clients. You have a lot of promise. If you wanted, you could obtain a license and do this kind of work full-time. I'm willing to help."

Erika's cynicism got the best of her. Elliott had trained her well.

"Why are you so willing to help a destitute woman when I'm sure you have young and carefree college students beating down your door for internships?"

There, she had said it. As soon as she had, however, she got a sinking feeling.

He might just realize I have a point and fire me tomorrow.

Derrick eased her doubts.

"Why not? Everyone needs a chance to make it," he said matter-of-factly. "If you're good, you deserve a chance."

He rose from the seat and picked up a small red bag filled with purple tissue paper that he had set on the floor without Erika noticing. He handed it to her.

"This is for you," he said. "The baby will get plenty of gifts today, but you deserve something special too."

He looked down at her and smiled.

"It was nice to meet you—again—Erika. I'm looking forward to working with you."

Near the end of the two-hour party, Erika opened her gifts. There were baby blankets and T-shirts and gift certificates for diapers and the baby supply superstore. Because she had shared with many of the shelter residents that she was having a boy, some of them had purchased blue or yellow outfits. Kathy gave her an IOU for babysitting. Erika was overwhelmed that a houseful of women who had so little had found a way to give so much.

Derrick's gift, which she opened last, was greeted with oohs and aahs. He had given her a gold watch with a thin band of gold intertwined with silver and a note card that read, "Erika, everything beautiful happens in its own time. Welcome to the staff of D. Haven Interior Designs. We hope you'll be open to what we can teach you about the design business and that, in our working relationship, we'll also learn from you."

"You guys didn't have to do this for me," Erika said softly.

"Don't tell us what to do or not to do, Ms. Wilson," Gabrielle said, feigning indignation.

At the end of the evening, Erika was spent. The residents moved all the gifts into her new first-floor bedroom and stacked them in a corner.

Erika settled in a kitchen chair and watched silently as Charlotte bustled about, putting away food, washing dishes, and humming the hymn she had been singing the night she picked Erika up from the train station.

"What is that?" Erika asked.

"What?"

"That song you're singing. You were singing it the night you brought me to the shelter."

Charlotte looked at her and smiled.

"It's an old gospel tune by Luther Barnes and the Red Budd Gospel Choir called 'I'm Still Holding On.'"

She sang a few lines.

"They said I wouldn't make it. They said I wouldn't be here today. But I'm still holding on to . . . his hand."

Erika closed her eyes and massaged her temples for a few minutes. When she looked up, Charlotte was still standing at the sink, gazing at her with concern.

"You okay?"

Erika's voice quivered as she responded.

"Let's see, I'm about to give birth to my first child, and I live in a shelter for battered women. I haven't worked in almost five years, and I have limited skills and limited resources for raising this baby. I'm just a little overwhelmed, Charlotte. Maybe I should go back to Elliott. At least I know we'll be taken care of."

Charlotte walked over to the table and pulled out a chair. She sat next to Erika and covered Erika's hands with her own.

"You're letting fear gnaw at you, aren't you? You're ready to give up because you're afraid of the unknown.

"Erika, I can't promise you that life is going to get any easier or be better than it is for you right now. But you already know that if you go back, you'll be your husband's prisoner—unless he kills you. Do you want that for your baby?"

She tried to peer into Erika's eyes, but Erika looked away.

"That's my other problem," Erika whispered. "I can't keep this baby, and I don't know what to do."

22

"T his is the day that the Lord has made. I will rejoice and be glad in it!"

Micah made that declaration under his breath as he walked swiftly from what, for the moment, was still his church study to the morning worship service.

He had prayed this morning for two hours before leaving home. Thirty minutes before the service began, he had locked the door to the study and knelt again, his elbows resting on the leather chair from which he had counseled and prayed with many members and rendered decisions he believed were in the best interest of his beloved church.

This morning, though, his spirit was heavy from the doubt and contempt he knew awaited him in the sanctuary. He wasn't surprised to find the pews full, not only with Standing Rock members, but also with many others who had heard the rumors about his impending demise and wanted to witness how the event unfolded.

When Micah reached the pulpit and walked toward his seat just behind the lectern, Jason stood and shook his hand. He leaned in and hugged Micah and patted his back.

"Good morning, Pastor," he whispered in Micah's ear.

Micah knew it looked to others as if Jason were giving him words of encouragement.

A modern-day Judas, he thought.

As Micah took his seat, and as Sister Gardner belted out the hymn "His Eye Is on the Sparrow," Micah's heart settled. He believed those lyrics.

He knew God had given him the message he would deliver this morning and that his heavenly Father's eyes were on him. Pops had returned to Oklahoma, but he was here in spirit too.

When Micah stood before the congregation, he skipped the usual lighthearted banter he sometimes used to engage them. After solemnly greeting the crowd, he glanced at Serena, who sat in the front pew in the center aisle for the first time ever since he had become pastor of the church. She smiled at him, with her lips and with her eyes.

Micah bowed for a brief word of prayer before launching into the text he had prepared.

"Your bulletins say we are going to continue our sermon series on what it takes to secure a blessing from God. For nearly nine months, I have taught and preached about God's willingness to grant us favor and prosper us. I had intended to wrap up this series a long time ago, but according to the bulletin, this series of sermons should take us into summer."

Micah continued as members of the congregation hung on his every word. Serena leaned forward in her seat.

"Standing Rock, preaching about God's goodness is

important. We need to know that we serve a good and generous Master who is ready and willing to bless us. But for the past few weeks, God has been telling me to share another message. Now is the time for this church to focus on serving others.

"If we'll take our eyes off of our wants and desires, God will anoint our work and reward us for showing his love to others.

"My heart has been heavy as I have watched daily news reports about young black men and boys killing each other in the streets of this city. I have been praying without ceasing for a family friend who is somewhere in hiding trying to put her life back together. I am troubled when I walk this neighborhood during the week to get lunch and see folks begging for money to feed their drug habits or for a sandwich to fill their bellies.

"God has pricked my conscience with the understanding that it is selfish to talk about prospering when so many others are simply trying to make do."

The thick silence in the sanctuary was punctuated by the piercing, thin cry of a newborn somewhere in the rear. Micah glanced at the deacons but shifted his gaze when he saw several of them glaring at him.

"I know this isn't easy to hear this morning, and these aren't easy words for me to speak," Micah continued. "But God told me that if we are to please him, to be granted the favor and prosperity we long for, we must begin to make a difference in the neighborhood surrounding this church. We must serve our fellow man from a pure heart.

"With that said, please turn with me to Matthew 22:35–39."

Micah delved into the text that explained the importance of loving others. Rather than the usual round of "Amens," his message was met mostly with stony silence and a few grunts here and there. Serena gave him an encouraging smile.

He ended with a plea for members of the congregation to put their differences aside and work together to show the least, the lost, and the lonely the unconditional love of God.

"I know you've heard this before, but it's true: sometimes the only God other people see is the God in you and me."

Micah was halfway up the aisle leading to the front of the church when someone tapped him on the shoulder.

"There's one more guest to greet before you check out of here, brother."

Micah thought he recognized the voice and turned quickly to see who was speaking to him.

"Ian Miller! Man, what are you doing here?"

The two men laughed and hugged.

"If you didn't have that preacher robe on, I'd pick you up like I used to in our frat house days."

They did their secret fraternity handshake and slapped one another on the back.

Two females approached and stood to the side as Micah and Ian completed their greeting. Ian finally turned toward them but continued speaking with Micah.

"Micah, you are an awesome preacher. When you chucked your medical career to go into the ministry, I thought you had lost your mind. But God is really using you. Your sermon really spoke to me today."

Micah smiled.

"Thanks, man. At least one person got it, huh? And what are you doing here in Richmond?"

Micah turned toward the two females.

"Bethany? And is this who used to be 'little' Victoria?"

Bethany extended her hand and pursed her lips.

"Good to see you too, Micah. The worship service was . . . intriguing."

Micah raised an eyebrow but didn't respond.

"How old are you now, Victoria?"

She was as tall as her mother and reed thin, with clear braces.

"I just turned fourteen," she said shyly.

Micah folded his arms and shook his head in disbelief.

"The last time I saw you, you were about seven or eight. You guys come with me to my study. I want you to say hello to Serena."

As they walked, Ian explained how his family had wound up in Richmond.

"We have moved here from Charlotte. I was promoted to senior VP of the mortgage division for Allegiance Bank's mid-Atlantic region, and the main office is here in Richmond."

Bethany interjected with an air of self-importance, "While he's working so hard at the office, my job is to take care of Victoria and our home."

"To be a shopaholic is more like it," Ian joked as Micah led the way to his study.

Serena was surprised when she saw the Millers. Ian enveloped her in a hug before she could speak.

She hadn't seen him or Bethany since she and Micah had wed. Ian, Micah's college roommate, had been a groomsman. She was meeting Victoria for the first time, because the girl hadn't attended the wedding.

And Bethany was here, as usual, prim and proper and turning up her nose. Serena extended her hand instead of offering a hug.

"Bethany, nice to see you."

Bethany nodded and lightly shook Serena's hand.

"What are you all doing in town? Why didn't you call us?" Serena asked Ian. "You could have stayed with us!" Bethany answered.

"We just bought a seven-bedroom house in Cheshire Lakes."

Ian jumped in before Bethany could say any more.

"My job transferred me here about a month ago, Serena. We bought the house and moved in about two weeks ago, but we wanted to surprise you and Micah. We're Richmonders too! Hopefully, we'll be getting together often, and coming to church."

Bethany coughed and looked at her manicured nails.

Ian tried to smooth over the awkward silence by continuing the conversation.

"Maybe you can show Bethany and Victoria around, get them plugged into the community."

Serena nodded and smiled at Bethany. She tried not to suck her teeth. This was going to be interesting.

"I'd be happy to do that, Bethany," she said. "Let me know when you want to get together."

Bethany flashed a perfect set of pearly whites and smiled sweetly at Serena.

"Well, I'm available anytime, you know. When I'm not playing tennis with the ladies in my neighborhood, I'm free. You do know where the quality malls are, don't you?

"And as far as Victoria, I guess you can't help me with activities for her. Most people who don't have children don't have a clue about their needs or interests."

Serena tried to keep her smile from fading.

Who made you God's gift to the world?

"I'm sure we can manage something, Bethany."

Serena walked over to Micah and took his hand.

"I know you're tired," she said. "You always are after a sermon. Let's go. Are Ian and his family joining us for dinner?"

She prayed fervently that the answer was no. Two minutes in the same room with Bethany had already tested her faith.

Ian shook his head. Serena was struck by his resemblance to Micah in complexion, height, and mannerisms, and if Serena hadn't known better, she would have thought they were brothers.

"Thanks for being so gracious, Serena, but not today. We just wanted to drop in and say hello and let you know that we're in town and we hope to see you guys more often."

He gave Micah and Serena hugs before leading his wife and daughter toward the door.

When they had gone, Serena rolled her eyes.

"It took everything within me not to do that in that

woman's face, Reverend," she told Micah. "She is something else."

Micah laughed.

"Don't let her worry you with all her airs. If Ian loves her, we can at least tolerate her. Let's go home, love. I know you're tired."

Neither of them had been sleeping well since Elliott had begun calling the house again and leaving threatening messages for Serena. She had tried to tell him she had no idea where Erika was, but he wasn't trying to hear it.

Serena kissed Micah's lips and grabbed her purse. As they walked toward their car, her imagination took over. Maybe she could give Elliott Bethany's phone number. Those two deserved each other.

23

Micah pulled out of the church parking lot and glanced at his wife.

"You feel like cooking? Why don't we go to the Hill Café? I could use a little something different today."

The cozy restaurant with ribs, roast, and other American cuisine in Richmond's Church Hill neighborhood was just right for a Sunday afternoon.

"That's fine, babe," Serena said and leaned her head back on the seat.

She closed her eyes as Micah drove, willing away the feelings of despair that were threatening to engulf her.

"What is it?" Micah asked as he weaved in and out of traffic. "Was my sermon that bad?"

Few people had approached him after the service to shake his hand or talk with him. Those who had ventured forth had seemed reluctant to do so in front of everyone else. Others had been defiant, willing someone to question them. Jason had left the pulpit without uttering good-bye.

Serena opened her eyes and looked at Micah. He looked

like a little boy who had lost his best friend. She reached over and stroked his cheek with the back of her hand.

"I love you, Micah."

"So the sermon *was* bad."

Serena laughed.

"I didn't know you cared so much what I thought, Reverend. I thought all that stuff was between you and 'Daddy.' As long as he's happy with you, all is well, right?"

Before Micah could retort, Serena's cell phone rang. She pulled it from her tiny red purse and read the numbers on the display.

"It's Melvin," she said.

She connected the call on speakerphone.

"Hello?"

"Hello, Serena."

"Hey, Melvin, how are you?"

"Doing great, Serena. How are you and Micah holding up?"

Serena glanced at her husband, who was listening.

"As well as can be expected, I guess. What's up?"

"Althea made enough gumbo this morning to feed the Richmond Braves. Since she doesn't personally know anyone on the baseball team, we thought we'd invite you and Micah over to help us polish it off."

He and Serena laughed together.

"We've just pulled up to the Hill Café," Serena said. "But I appreciate the invitation. Thank Althea for me and tell her don't forget us next time."

"Will do, will do," Melvin said. He paused before continuing. "Actually, I was hoping you guys would be able to come by. I wanted to talk with Micah and see how he's holding up."

Serena smiled. Melvin was showing another side of himself these days.

"Want to speak to him?"

She passed the phone to Micah, who had been fiddling with his CDs.

Micah took the cell, which was still on speakerphone mode, and gave Serena a curious look. Serena knew he was wondering what was up; he and Melvin had never called one another before.

"'Lo?"

"Micah, how ya doing, son?"

Micah paused.

"I'm not sure. Word is spreading, huh?"

Melvin paused.

"It doesn't matter," Micah continued. "Deacons talk. Church folk talk. Most of the congregation was at that meeting the trustee board called the other night."

"I've heard the probably inaccurate story circulating, Micah, but in the past few years, I've had the privilege of getting to know you. I've never doubted your integrity, your faith, or your commitment to serving God. Whatever the problem is, continue to do as God is leading you, son. Even if everyone at Standing Rock Community Church turns against you, God is standing with you."

Micah tightened his grip on the cell phone but didn't reply.

Seeming to understand, Melvin asked to speak to Serena.

"Thanks, Melvin," Micah said gruffly.

He gave the cell phone back to Serena and averted his gaze when he opened the door to the Audi. Serena followed him with her eyes until he disappeared inside the cozy single-story building to see if there was a waiting list.

"Hey there," Serena said to Melvin after turning off the speakerphone mode and cradling the phone close to her ear. "Got any weapons over there I can use on these trifling church folk we're dealing with?"

Melvin laughed.

"You should know by now that we're all trifling—maybe in different ways, but we've all got issues, ma'am."

Serena sighed.

"Don't I know it."

She fell silent as her thoughts turned again to the baby it seemed she was never going to have.

"What is it?" Melvin asked.

"Melvin, have you ever wanted something so bad that it consumed your every thought?" Serena didn't wait for him to answer. "I don't think I'm ever going to be a mother, at least not the natural way. I'm just trying to figure out how to deal with this and not be mad at God."

"I understand, Serena. I've been there. That's how we wound up adopting Kami. We love your two half brothers, but for some reason we couldn't conceive again. Believe it or not, even after you have children, dealing with infertility can be hard."

Serena took a deep breath to hold back the tears. She had done enough crying lately.

"I've had two ectopic pregnancies, shot myself in the butt and hips with all kinds of fertility drugs, stood on my head to make sure the sperm could find my eggs, and anything else ridiculous you could think of. But still no baby. Still no baby."

She started giggling as she thought about all the advice she had followed.

"And get this: when we finally have enough money saved and the insurance company gives their approval to move forward with in vitro fertilization, Micah comes home with the news that he might be out of a job and we might need the money to pay our mortgage. I didn't know God had such an interesting sense of humor."

She laughed again, but the tears were closer to the surface.

"I wish I had the answers, Serena," Melvin said. "Some things we just have to live with, trusting that God knows best. I'll tell you this, though. If money is your only obstacle, that can be resolved. There's more than fifty thousand dollars sitting in an account with your name on it that you refused to accept to pay for grad school almost ten years ago."

Serena was stunned. She pulled the cell phone away from her ear and looked at it.

Am I hearing things?

She put the phone back to her ear.

"Excuse me, Melvin? What did you just say?"

He repeated himself, this time talking more slowly.

"I didn't mean to tell you under these circumstances, Serena, but this money is yours. I started the fund when you were born and occasionally pulled from it when you were growing up to help your mother with some of your extracurricular activities and school expenses.

"I've known that when the time was right, I could tell

163

you about it and offer it to you. It's your money, Serena. Spend it as you like."

Micah had returned to the car and opened her door.

"They have a table ready for us," he mouthed when he saw she was still on the phone.

Serena felt as if she were in the twilight zone. She put her palm up for Micah to wait.

"Melvin, I don't know what to say. I mean, I don't know how to say this without sounding rude, but I can't—"

Melvin cut her off.

"Serena, don't say any more right now. Like I said, I only told you about this because the time seems right. I'm not trying to buy your love or pay you off or relieve any guilt. I've made my peace with God, and hopefully, the friendship between you and me will deepen. That's all I want. I'll send you the account information tomorrow."

Before she could say any more, Melvin ended the conversation.

"Your husband is waiting for you. I know you must be starving. Don't fret about this; just take your time. Give me a call and let me know how you and Micah are doing."

Serena climbed out of the car and stood next to the waiting Micah.

"Melvin . . . thank you."

24

Before she could talk herself out of it, Erika took the cell phone Charlotte had offered her and locked the door to Charlotte's office. She sat at Charlotte's desk and stared at the telephone keypad for the longest time.

Can I really do this? Can I ask someone I've betrayed to help me out like this?

Erika looked at her growing belly and saw the baby kick. She felt it too and rubbed the spot just above her navel where part of her son's foot protruded.

She loved this baby already. She couldn't wait to hold him, to kiss him. But could she give him up, even temporarily? The thought of doing so made her feel guilty, as if she were already repeating her mother's pattern of abandoning one's child for selfish gain.

Charlotte had encouraged her to look at the big picture.

"You're not giving him up for adoption, Erika. You need some help to get on your feet. Your internship with D. Haven Interior Designs is going well; they're willing to keep you on to teach you the ropes and even help you prepare for your license. You couldn't ask for a better opportunity. If you'll concentrate on succeeding at this, you'll be able to do something you love and financially support your son with no problems.

"Whom do you trust to take your baby, love him, and willingly return him to your care once you've gotten established?"

Serena had immediately come to mind when she and Charlotte had had that conversation after the baby shower three days ago. Serena might find it hard to let go, but she would do the right thing; she would honor a promise to Erika.

"How can I ask her to do this for me after I stood her up at her wedding?" Erika had asked. "And what if Elliott sees the baby and figures out that it's his? He'll take my child, and I'll never see him again."

Charlotte took the conversation to the place she always did: her faith.

"If this Serena is as wonderful and as faithful as you describe her, she'll receive you with open arms. Her emails to you have indicated as much, haven't they?"

Erika agreed.

"Serena has been known to hold a grudge! I couldn't believe how she cut her mother off for years because of some issue they had. But Serena's big heart always overrules that stubbornness. She really is a good person."

Charlotte leaned back in her chair and smiled at Erika.

"Sounds like it. None of us is perfect. Thank God for still using wounded people, or we wouldn't stand a chance to be blessed or to share our faith with others. Before you make this decision, though, let's make sure you've explored all of your other options. What about your mother?"

"I wouldn't leave a stuffed animal in her care," Erika replied with a straight face.

"What about your other relatives? An aunt or grandmother?"

"Because we traveled so often and my mother's family questioned her lifestyle, I was never close to any of my relatives. It was mostly Mom and me, and I pretty much raised myself because she was so busy with her latest romantic conquest.

"By the time I really got to know my grandmother and my mom's two sisters, I was in high school and had insisted on settling down somewhere to graduate. Aunt Sheila was wonderful. She was an elementary school principal and really encouraged me to buckle down in my studies so I could get a college degree. If it weren't for her, I probably wouldn't have one.

"According to my mother, my father was an alcoholic who barely knew my name. He and my mother never married, so I never really got to know his family."

Erika sighed and gazed at the ceiling as she reconnected with her memories.

"Aunt Sheila died of breast cancer during my sophomore year in college. Elliott went to the funeral with me and was so sweet and tender. My grandmother took Aunt Sheila's death hard.

"She fell and broke her hip not too long after that and wound up in a nursing home. She passed away the year I graduated from Commonwealth University."

Charlotte leaned forward and grasped her hand.

167

"I know this is hard. When you're bringing a baby into the world, the thing you want most is to cling to your family. When there's no one there to support you and help you celebrate, part of you grieves and part of you is terrified. But you and the baby will get through this and form your own beautiful family. I'm already part of it."

Erika ignored the tears coursing down her cheeks and stretched her arms toward Charlotte for a hug.

Charlotte gave it to her and laughed.

"That basketball attached to your stomach is in the way, and I think the little athlete kicked me!"

Erika sat back and laughed.

"Join the club!"

They had prayed together yesterday, and before Charlotte left for home, she had given Erika her cell phone.

"You know the rules. You can't let anyone know where you are or use our office phones because caller ID is a danger. We don't want anyone tracing your calls.

"But you don't need to be waddling to the convenience store down the block, trying to get change for that pay phone downstairs. Use my cell to call Serena. If she has caller ID, she'll realize you're in the D.C. area, but under these circumstances, we need to make sure she can be trusted anyway. She's got to meet you at some point to pick up the baby."

Erika had tucked the phone inside the duffle bag she often carried with her copy of *What to Expect When You're Expecting*, a bottle of water, and more recently, a small Bible Charlotte had given her. It translated the Scriptures into easy-to-understand language and had helpful commentaries in the margins.

Erika had been restless most of last night, trying to get comfortable between her trips to the bathroom. Each time she would get up, she would glance at the duffle bag and be tempted to pull out the phone and call.

What would Serena say? And Micah? What would they think of her for even asking?

This morning she had awakened just before dawn and prayed silently as she lay in her bed on her left side, stroking her stomach.

Erika was filled with a peace she had never felt before. Was this what it meant to have a relationship with God, to let him lead your life?

Somehow she knew everything would work out. It wasn't going to be easy, but it would be okay.

Before she could change her mind, she had risen from the bed and put on her robe and those pink slippers she had worn for months now.

When I leave this place, I'm taking these slippers with me to always remind myself of where I've been and how far I can go, she had told herself.

Just the thought of there being a someday in which she could have that conversation with herself bolstered her courage.

She had grabbed Charlotte's cell phone and found the folded piece of white paper that contained an email reply from Serena in which Serena had provided her work, home, and cell phone numbers.

Now she sat at Charlotte's desk, glancing at the clock. It was seven o'clock. Serena was probably getting ready for a Monday morning meeting at the office. She hoped her friend wasn't going to work before daylight like she used to when she had been an up-and-comer at Turner One Advertising.

Erika held her breath as she made a call that could change both of their lives.

25

In her previous job, Serena had begun to dread Monday mornings. They meant the beginning of a new week to submit fresh ideas for the next big campaign. Serena had loved the advertising world, the need to be creative, and the high-energy team she worked with, but the deadlines and the competitiveness could be draining. Monday mornings at Turner One had been akin to a weeklong prep for the Miss America pageant or the Super Bowl.

Since taking the helm of the Children's Art Coalition, she felt like she was on a perpetual vacation. The adage that if you love your work it won't seem like work was so true.

Serena had found her niche in using her artistic and creative abilities to help underprivileged children thrive. Not only did the work have meaning, it also was fun. And it meant she could have a leisurely Monday morning cup of coffee with her husband. She didn't have to rush to the office to make sure she didn't miss an important call or to prepare the latest and greatest presentation for a corporate client who, depending on his mood that day, might love it or hate it.

Serena rose from bed and slid into her lilac silk robe before padding to the bathroom to brush her teeth. Micah was already there, standing over his sink, shaving.

"You're up early today, Rev," she said and rubbed his back. "I would kiss you, but I bet your teeth are already clean."

He faked a frown.

"Yes, please brush first."

He returned to shaving and tried to answer her at the same time.

"Got a meeting this morning with the church staff. A planning session for Vacation Bible School."

Serena swished warm water around in her mouth to rinse her teeth. She dabbed her lips with a soft towel before responding.

"No word from anyone on yesterday's sermon?"

Micah shook his head.

"Any word on the status of the contract with the PGU Gospel Network?"

Micah shook his head again, put his razor down, and looked at his wife.

"I'm just on staff now, Serena. They've shut me out as much as they can. But I bet Jason Lyons knows the answers to those questions. I'm just wondering if I've done the right thing."

The phone rang. Serena reached for the cordless receiver attached to the wall.

"Don't second guess yourself, Micah."

She put the receiver to her ear.

172

"Hello?"

"Serena, is that you?"

Serena laid her damp washcloth on the edge of the sink and pressed the phone closer to her ear.

"Erika?" she whispered. "Is that you?"

"Yeah, it's me," came the soft reply. "It's me."

"I've been getting your emails every so often. How are you? Where are you? Do you need me to come?"

Erika was silent on the other end of the phone. When Serena heard the sniffling, she realized her sister-friend was crying.

"Whatever it is, it's okay, E. I'm here."

Erika managed to laugh through her tears.

"Ha," she said thickly. "You might take those words back when you find out why I'm calling."

Serena remained silent, waiting.

"I can't tell you where I am, Serena, but I need your help. I'm about to have my baby in a few weeks, and I can't handle motherhood right now."

Erika broke down again. As she sobbed, Serena did too.

"Sh, E. It's okay, it's okay. Whatever you need, just tell me."

Erika managed to compose herself long enough to choke out her request.

"Serena, I know we haven't talked in nearly four years, but I also know that you are a good and loving person. I have no right to ask you this, and I don't even know what's going on in your life right now, but if you can find it in your heart, and if Micah is willing, I need you to take my baby for a while."

Serena gasped.

Is this your answer, God? To bless me with someone else's baby? I want my own child! If I take this baby in, what about my plans to get pregnant?

Serena was startled by the ferocity of her own selfishness.

She heard the answer immediately.

"Give, and it will be given to you: good measure, pressed down, shaken together, and running over will be put into your bosom. For with the same measure that you use, it will be measured back to you."

Shame flooded her heart. No matter what it cost her, she knew what she was going to do. She didn't have to ask her husband. She knew he would agree.

"Erika, don't worry. Your baby has a home here. I will love him or her like my own and make sure that when you're ready, your baby will return to you healthy and happy."

She could feel the weight of worry lifting from Erika's shoulders.

"What about Micah? Do you need to check with him first?"

"Erika, can you hold on? I'll ask him now."

Serena, who had sat on the small wicker chair in a corner of the bathroom, rose and padded across the carpeted floor of the bathroom to Micah, who stood at the sink, wiping the remnants of shaving cream from his now-smooth jawline.

She put the phone on mute and leaned against the sink for support. Micah looked at her in the mirror and turned to face her when he saw tears coursing down her cheeks.

"What is it, love?"

Concern filled his face when he saw her sad eyes.

"I have Erika on the phone, so I'll give you the Cliff's Notes version," she said quickly. "First of all, Melvin told me yesterday that he has fifty thousand dollars sitting in an account with my name on it. He says I can use it for the in vitro procedure or for whatever I choose. I was going to tell you later tonight so we could pray about what to do."

She waved the cordless phone at Micah.

"Erika is about to have the baby but is still living in the shelter and needs some help. She wants us to take the baby until she gets on her feet. She wants to know if you'll agree."

Micah looked as if he'd seen a ghost. Serena knew she had slammed him with more than enough news to send him running to his home office to spend the rest of the day in prayer and contemplation. In the almost four years she had been his wife, she had seen how he processed things. But time was of the essence.

She stood pensively before him, waiting. Micah slid the phone from her hand and clicked off the mute button.

"Erika, your baby will be safe here with us. We'll love your little one as our own."

Serena leaned into him and laid her head on his shoulder as he asked Erika when the baby would be born. The tears kept coming.

This was the second time God had put a major obstacle in the way of her undergoing in vitro fertilization. Was he trying to send her a message? Right now would be a good time to get a word from him.

Micah rubbed Serena's back and gave her the phone.

Erika told her how Charlotte would help her deliver her son and how she planned to nurse him for six weeks before sending him to Richmond.

"I need you and Micah to care for him while I work to get on my feet. I have an internship with an interior design firm that's willing to help me get certified in this field, but I've got to pay my dues. I've got to put in the time in order to be ready to study for my license.

"This isn't an easy decision, you know," Erika said and paused.

Serena tried to pull herself together. She could tell Erika needed reassurance, validation.

"I know, Erika. It can't be. But in making it, you're showing how much you love your baby."

"I do love this baby, even though he's not here yet," Erika said firmly. "And Serena, I want him back. It might take me a year or so to get myself together and save some money and move out of this shelter, but I will do it. I want to raise my son."

"We understand." Serena said. "We're here to help, but we know that this child is yours. You can trust us."

"Whatever you do," Erika responded, "Elliott can't find out about this. He would take the baby and run just to get back at me."

Serena looked at her husband before she spoke.

"We won't tell Elliott. We don't want to jeopardize your safety or the baby's."

Serena looked into Micah's eyes to make sure they were in agreement: Erika didn't need to know that Elliott still called Serena regularly, demanding information on

Erika's whereabouts, or that he sometimes watched their house.

When Elliott had parked a block away one afternoon last week, Micah had walked down the sloping driveway, crossed two streets, and confronted him.

Elliott had stood his ground; he was convinced that Serena knew where Erika was and he wanted to know too, Micah told Serena later.

Micah recounted the incident for Serena when he returned home.

"I told him if he had treated Erika like a wife instead of a punching bag, he wouldn't be sitting in our neighborhood like Columbo or Kojak," Micah said. "I told him to stop harassing you and to get some help."

Elliott had snapped and started spewing curses, Micah said. "I thought I was looking at a different person."

Serena had stood in the window of her home, watching the exchange and worrying that Elliott might do something crazy like pull a gun on her husband. She had clutched the cordless phone in her hand, preparing to call 911 if Elliott made any moves toward Micah.

She thought about that incident today as she reassured her best friend that the baby would be safe from its father.

Erika ended the conversation by promising to call when the baby was born and designate a time and place to meet so she could hand over her son. As she said those words, her voice trembled again.

"E, I love you. We're in this together."

Serena made sure Erika had her cell phone number,

and gave her Micah's, before hanging up and falling into her husband's arms.

"It's wonderful to hear from her, so why do I feel so bad? Why am I jealous that she's pregnant and I'm not?" she asked softly.

She thanked God she had married a man who, although a preacher, never judged her humanness.

Micah stroked his wife's hair and held her tight.

"Too bad life isn't perfect," he murmured. "We'll deal with this, and we'll be fine."

26

Micah arrived at Standing Rock promptly at nine o'clock, prepared for whatever the morning would bring. Or so he thought.

When he reached his office, his key wouldn't work. He jiggled and twisted the doorknob and knocked to see if someone was inside playing a prank.

"Have they locked me out already?" he said aloud in jest.

"Yes, we have, Rev. McDaniels."

Micah turned to find Deacon Ames standing in the middle of the hallway, holding a ring full of keys and wearing a smug smile.

"Excuse me?" Micah stood next to the door and waited for Deacon Ames to approach him.

"We had a packed-house church meeting last night, Reverend," Deacon Ames said. Micah noticed that he was no longer using the word *Pastor*.

"The vote to remove you from the leadership position of this church was twelve hundred to nine hundred. Jason Lyons will immediately begin his duties as senior pastor.

You have an hour to clean out any personal belongings you want to take with you, while I supervise."

Deacon Ames extended an ivory linen envelope to Micah.

"This is your formal termination letter and three months of severance. We've appreciated how far you've brought Standing Rock, but your vision and the church's seem to be on different trajectories. It's time for us to move in a new direction."

Micah stared at the deacon who had pursued him earnestly to be the pastor of Standing Rock nearly five years ago. He refused to take the envelope.

"Tell me, Deacon Ames, when does the first episode of Standing Rock air on the PGU Gospel Network? What kind of deadline are you racing to meet?"

Deacon Ames turned his head.

"Take the envelope," he said with his teeth clenched.

Deacon Ames released the envelope. Micah stepped back and let it hit the floor. His gaze remained on Deacon Ames, waiting for him to make eye contact.

When Deacon Ames finally looked at him, Micah said, "So this is it? No one had the decency to invite me to a meeting at the church I lead? Or to call me and at least tell me the news before I showed up today?"

Deacon Ames looked away again and fiddled with the keys in his hand until he found the new key to Micah's former office.

"Come on in," he said as he walked in. "And don't leave that letter and check on the floor."

Micah remained in the doorway.

Was this really happening? Was this all the respect he

deserved after serving this congregation with his heart and soul?

He wanted to enter the office and retrieve his personal files, but he also wanted to take his pride right out the door. He knew he had some legal ground to stand on. Since he had not been invited to the meeting at church, he could probably fight the members' vote.

Prudence won. As Deacon Ames stood to the side of the massive desk, guarding the office like it held bricks of gold, Micah retrieved his Rolodex and the files containing his sermons. He took several starched white shirts from the small closet in the corner and photos of Serena and extended family from the desk.

There was no box waiting, which surprised him. He gathered as much as he could in his arms and walked toward the door.

Micah looked at Deacon Ames, who was surveying his manicured nails. He scanned the office one final time.

"Deacon Ames," Micah said, forcing the man to look up at him. "May God be with you and with this church. You can mail me that letter and my severance check whenever you decide, after you pick it up from the floor."

With that, he slowly walked down the long hallway to the side entrance of Standing Rock. When he reached the door, he uttered a prayer.

"Lord, I know you would never forsake me. I know that even now you are with me. Keep me strong. Help me to remember the many ways you have brought me through before. Help me to keep my head high and know that I am your child and you love me, no matter what."

Micah leaned on the door with his arms, which were

laden with his belongings, and stepped into the sunny morning. How was he going to go home and tell his already grief-stricken wife that what they had been dreading had finally happened—he no longer had a job?

It was a new day, in more ways than one.

27

Gabrielle eased her gold Lexus into the circular driveway and parked between a Mercedes and a BMW. She turned to look at Erika.

"Ready to go in and meet a new client?"

Erika peered at the salmon brick Georgetown residence. Ready or not, she had to take the plunge if she was serious about becoming an interior designer. This was the first time Gabrielle had invited her along to work with a long-term, A-list client, and she wasn't about to blow the opportunity.

She glanced at the bulge protruding beneath the starched teal, white, and beige striped, collared shirt she wore under her khaki blazer and bit her lip. Gabrielle patted her shoulder.

"You look great, Erika. I must say, you have good taste when it comes to clothes, even maternity wear."

At her baby shower, Gabrielle had given Erika a generous gift certificate to an upscale online maternity store so she could purchase outfits to wear to meetings with clients. Erika had completed her khaki business-casual look with dangling gold earrings and low-heeled tan sling-back pumps.

Her hair was pulled back into a bun, making her fuller, yet still gorgeous, honey-toned face appear more mature. She looked like a stylish, elegant, and capable designer who happened to be with child.

Erika smiled sheepishly at Gabrielle.

"Thanks for the compliment, and thanks again for the gift certificate. You can tell I'm nervous, huh? I'll be fine," Erika said.

Gabrielle nodded and opened her door to step out of the car.

"I wanted you to feel your best these last few weeks before the baby comes, as you start meeting some of our regular clients. Once you resume your work after the baby's born, you'll be able to make follow-up calls or visits for the company, and the clients will be comfortable with you."

Erika slowly emerged from the passenger seat and waddled around to the sidewalk until she was standing next to Gabrielle, with her sleek figure, tailored pantsuit, and one-inch heels. At thirty-six, Gabrielle was just a few years older than Erika, but Erika felt like a much younger, dowdy kindergartner venturing to school for the first time with her beautiful older sister at her side.

Gabrielle gave her a once-over and winked at her. She glanced at Erika's hand and smiled approvingly. She had advised Erika to put on her wedding ring to avoid raising any questions among their clients about Erika's marital status.

Gabrielle took pains to slow her pace as she walked with Erika up the brick walkway, which was bordered on the left and right by low-lying shrubs, fresh mulch, and pink and yellow tulips.

An iron bench sat to the left of the doorway under a small awning, providing shade and a respite for the owners when, or if, they ever chose to sit in their front yard and watch passersby. As Gabrielle rang the doorbell to the early-twentieth-century colonial, Erika surmised that these owners rarely took that opportunity. The seat seemed more for show than for regular use.

The maid opened the door and ushered Gabrielle and Erika inside. Erika gasped before she could catch herself.

From the outside the house had looked somewhat modest, or at the least, nothing grand. But the expansive, richly hued foyer with cathedral ceilings told a different story.

The marble beneath Erika's feet gleamed. The deep red walls were lined with gold-gilded framed portraits of family members, including long-dead ancestors. Antique tables and armchairs that had likely been passed down for several generations, or had been purchased to appear so, made the space cozy.

I wonder if Gabrielle designed this space, Erika thought.

The maid led her and Gabrielle to the living room and offered them something to drink.

"Mrs. Winchester will come down shortly," she said softly in a lyrical accent that Erika couldn't place.

When the maid had left the room, Erika gazed about, still overwhelmed by the beauty and elegance of her surroundings. The living room had been painted a deep shade of blue to contrast with the plush burgundy sofa on which she now sat. Artwork in this room included original paintings by impressionist artists that undoubtedly had been bought at an auction.

A sea of windows lined one wall, facing into a brick-fenced courtyard to the side of the house. Erika gazed at petunias, begonias, hostas, and other flowers and plants blooming there with abandon. There was also a birdbath that doubled as a fountain.

Gabrielle unpacked her briefcase, setting pertinent papers and design photos on the walnut coffee table before her. Her eyes followed Erika's to the courtyard, and she smiled as she sat back on the sofa to wait for Mrs. Winchester.

"Like it? That was one of the projects I helped pull together, along with the design and decoration of this room and the foyer."

"It's beautiful," Erika said.

"Thanks. This house has been gutted and renovated from top to bottom since Mr. and Mrs. Winchester bought it four years ago. It had much smaller rooms, with limited flow.

"D. Haven Interior Designs came in and assessed the couple's needs and preferences and determined that they would benefit from a grand yet functional living space. We took down a few walls, added more windows, and hired a landscaper to design this garden and the one out front."

And I thought the McMansion Elliott and I shared in Richmond was something, Erika mused.

She was awestruck but realized that she needed to pull herself together before Mrs. Winchester arrived. After all, she was part of the team preparing to continue the renovations.

They were here today to provide estimates for a home

office so Mrs. Winchester could better manage her numerous volunteer and charitable commitments. She also had decided she needed to revamp her kitchen and add a skylight so more sun could pour in.

Erika glanced at the sketches and specifications Gabrielle had placed on the coffee table, facing away from the two of them, in the direction from which Mrs. Winchester would be viewing them.

After another five minutes or so, a petite blond woman, at least two decades Gabrielle's senior but still very striking, glided into the room in a cocoon of sweet-scented perfume. She carried a glass of sherry in her left hand and reached up with her right arm to give Gabrielle a hug.

Mrs. Winchester extended her hand to Erika.

"I'm Zeta Gray Hutchinson Winchester. Pleased to make your acquaintance, my dear."

Her grip was strong. Erika tried to prevent a wince from replacing her smile and prayed that the woman would ease up before her fingers grew numb.

Is this where Gabrielle learned the woman-of-steel handshake? Erika wondered. *Lord, please don't let my hand muscles be crushed.*

When Mrs. Winchester released Erika's hand, she patted Erika's stomach and smiled.

"You and your husband are so lucky. Congratulations. Have you two decided on names for the little one?"

Erika glanced at Gabrielle, whose eyes warned her not to go there.

Erika smiled weakly.

"We're still tossing about many ideas, but we do know it's a boy."

Mrs. Winchester's eyes lit up. She took a sip of her sherry as she settled into an oversized sofa chair and motioned for Erika and Gabrielle to sit down again.

"You know, I've always loved the name Clarkson. But my husband and I had two daughters. They're both adults now, so whenever they settle down and pursue motherhood, maybe I can get one of them to select that name."

Erika smiled politely.

Gabrielle launched right into a presentation about the design options for the study. She paused strategically at several points to allow Erika a chance to comment or add her perspective on a particular element in the room.

"You can go with the bookcases lining the wall, which will give you a more formal study effect, or with three strategically placed armoires, which will give the room a more contemporary feel but hide the books when you're not searching your shelves," Erika said.

Mrs. Winchester nodded.

"I love these choices. You're good, young lady," she told Erika. "I know you and my dear friend Gabrielle collaborated on this, but I can see your spark. You're going to go far."

Erika blushed at the compliment. She was still getting used to people saying nice things about her. Had Elliott ever done that?

"Thank you, Mrs. Winchester. That means a lot. I enjoy the work."

Gabrielle took a sip of the Tahitian water the maid had set on a napkin on the table next to her.

"She has a good eye, Mrs. Winchester," Gabrielle said. "We bring the best onto our team."

"Then I'm looking forward to working with you again, Gabrielle, and with you for the first time, Erika," Mrs. Winchester said. "My husband always makes me get three estimates before I undertake a new project, but for some reason, I always keep coming back to D. Haven Interior Designs. Whatever it is, I haven't been disappointed yet. How soon can we get started?"

Before Gabrielle could respond, Erika gasped and clutched her stomach. At least thirty seconds passed before she was able to speak or react. The tightening across her lower abdomen was painful enough to take her breath away. When it had subsided, she took a deep breath and looked from Gabrielle to Mrs. Winchester.

"You two may have to move forward on this particular project without me, Mrs. Winchester. I'm having contractions."

28

Micah sat in the restaurant on Brown's Island, looking out of the panoramic window at the gently rolling James River. Professionals on their lunch breaks and women with children tucked in carriages and strollers walked leisurely along the riverbank.

Micah had considered calling Serena to cancel their lunch date—after all, he no longer had a steady paycheck. They should be saving every penny, especially with Erika's baby coming to live with them soon. But this was their special spot.

He and Serena had their first lunch date here seven years ago, soon after they met during a late-night fender bender. It was at this restaurant he had questioned Serena's commitment to her high-powered advertising career and the calling on her heart. It was here that an easy friendship had been formed.

Maybe it was fitting, then, that on a day when he had some life-changing news, he was in a place that reminded him of the love born in friendship he now shared with his wife. He had some difficult news for her, but because of their track record, he knew they'd weather this storm together.

The ice in Micah's glass clinked against the sides as he raised it to his lips and finished off his Pepsi. Serena's strawberry lemonade had already been served and was waiting at her spot at the table.

Lord, it's me in need of help now, he thought. *Are you here?*

Always, son. When you don't see me or feel me, it's because I'm carrying you, remember? Hold on for the ride.

Micah sighed.

I hope I'm strong enough. I hope I've made the right choices.

Micah heard the reply as clearly as if God was right there:

Keep your hope and trust in me.

When the waitress strolled by and dropped off another soda for Micah, Serena appeared. She glided toward her husband and smiled. He knew she loved meeting here; it always made her nostalgic and romantic. To top it off, she was looking lovely in purple. Today's shade of lavender complemented her cinnamon complexion.

Serena bent to lightly kiss Micah's lips before taking her seat across from him in the cozy booth.

"Hey, babe," she said as she removed the paper from her straw and plunged it into her lemonade.

"Mmm, this is good. How are you today?"

Micah tried to smile, but his eyes wouldn't cooperate. Concern crossed Serena's face. She reached across the table for his hands.

"What's wrong? Are they tripping again about this PGU broadcast?"

Micah heard the attitude in her voice as she began to speak more loudly. He raised his palm.

"Calm down, love," he said softly. "It's all good, because it's all God."

Serena sat back and folded her arms across her chest. Her brow furrowed with worry.

How am I going to tell her this? Micah asked himself.

I am with you, son.

Micah cleared his throat and put his elbows on the table. He extended his palms toward Serena, indicating that he wanted her to put her hands in his.

Serena leaned forward and complied.

"Whatever it is, Micah, I'm here," she whispered as she looked deeply into his eyes.

Micah nodded.

"I know, love. I know. When I went to the church this morning and tried to open the door to my study, the key wouldn't work. They've changed the locks and voted me out as pastor, Serena. Deacon Ames was waiting there for me with a formal letter of termination."

"What the—"

Micah put a finger to Serena's lips to stop her before she said something she would regret. Her eyes were flashing, and she had removed her hands from his and placed them on her hips.

"Micah, have they lost their minds? Is this a church or a corporation? They get rid of their pastor so they can be on TV? And God's supposed to be up in this? I know this has been a possibility, but I guess I thought they would come to their senses and try to work things out with you."

Micah rested his forehead in the palm of his hand.

"Maybe I'm wrong, Serena. Maybe I'm the only one with hang-ups about Standing Rock spreading its ministry via television. Tons of other churches do it with no problem. Maybe they were right to get rid of me so they could move forward. I just don't know."

Serena's eyes widened. She grabbed Micah's chin, forcing him to raise his head and look into her eyes.

"You've been going around and around about this for months, Micah," she said. "Maybe there's nothing wrong with a television ministry, but obviously that's not the ministry God has given you. He wants you to go in another direction. You have to follow where he leads. And I do too. We're in this together."

Micah leaned forward and kissed her tenderly, oblivious to the other lunchtime diners.

"Promise?"

Serena nodded as they clasped hands.

His ringing cell phone broke their reverie.

"Maybe it's Deacon Ames, asking me to return the Bible the church gave me when they installed me as pastor," Micah joked.

He was surprised when he looked at the view panel on the phone and saw that it actually was Deacon Ames's phone number.

"Micah here."

"Micah, Deacon Ames. We have an emergency and need your help."

Micah sat back in his seat, his mouth ajar.

"Am I hearing you correctly? It *was* you who informed me a few hours ago that I've been fired, right? Have you had a change of heart already?"

Micah could picture Deacon Ames bristling on the other end of the phone and rubbing his hand across his head as he often did when he was nervous or agitated.

"No, no change of heart. Just an emergency," he said curtly. "John Artis, that teenager you baptized last fall, was killed last night, not too far from Standing Rock. Police say it was a drive-by. His mother has insisted that you deliver the eulogy, since one of your sermons led the boy to give his life to Christ."

"John is dead?"

Micah stared at Serena, wishing the call were on speakerphone so he wouldn't have to repeat any of this for her.

Deacon Ames returned to the matter at hand.

"The funeral is scheduled for Thursday. Can you come and do the eulogy? We'll list you on the program as pastor and consider it your last official duty. Your three months of severance will include an additional three hundred dollars to reflect your service."

Micah couldn't believe the coldness in Deacon Ames's voice. Was it coming straight from his heart? Micah's mother was right as usual: people didn't change; they simply revealed who they really were.

"Don't worry about the money, Deacon Ames. I'll be there for this family. Please give me Ms. Artis's phone number. Serena and I will stop by there later today."

By the time he had completed the call, Serena had paid the bill and was placing a tip on the table for the waitress.

"I heard enough to know there's been a tragedy. I'll call Connie at the office and let her know I won't be returning today. Let's get to Ms. Artis."

194

29

Erika lay in the narrow hospital bed with the rails up on both sides and stared at the ceiling. Neither boring her eyes into the fluorescent lights nor breathing short, quick breaths during her contractions helped.

This pain just plain hurt. These contractions were no joke. Chewing ice didn't help. Neither did squeezing Charlotte's hand.

"Remind me why I'm not getting an epidural?" she asked Charlotte between breaths.

Charlotte smiled at her tenderly and rubbed her forehead.

"You're tired, aren't you? You're doing a great job, Erika. You really are. Just hang on."

Charlotte's soothing words helped.

Thank you, God, for sending her to me. Thank you for using her to lead me to you, Erika prayed silently.

I give good things to my children.

The contractions kept Erika from smiling, but she heard the Master. She knew he was here with her even though she was preparing to take this ride as a single mother and would soon be separated from her baby.

God's presence gave her a peace she couldn't explain even as she grieved over her circumstances.

She didn't want to be having her baby alone, without her husband at her side. She didn't want to be facing an uncertain future, unable to simply enjoy her son and spend her days watching him grow and smelling his sweet scent. Life was so unfair.

But even as another contraction seized her body and washed away coherency, Erika knew it wasn't that simple. She had played the notes of her life instrument. She had chosen this path, despite Serena's warnings and Elliott's track record of abuse. These were the consequences for her insecurity.

In overlooking Elliott's faults because the outer package had been appealing, she had repeated the same mistakes her mother had made with men time and time again. She was so determined to be different from her mother that she had stayed with Elliott even after realizing the extremely high cost.

Now here she was. Alone anyway. A single mother like her own mother had been.

But two things were different. She was getting counseling at the shelter to learn how to make better choices, to learn how to love herself. And for the first time in her life, she really believed there was a God and that he wasn't going to let anything terrible happen to her or this child.

Marcy, the energetic young nurse who was working the midnight shift, came in at the top of the hour to check Erika's vitals and see how much she had dilated.

"You doing okay?" she asked in a high-pitched, chipper voice that reminded Erika of an overzealous preschool teacher.

Marcy chuckled when Erika, irritated and just coming out of a contraction, snapped, "You tell me."

She looked over the top of the sheet at Erika after checking her cervix.

"Time to call Dr. Washington. You're ten centimeters. This baby is on its way."

30

Serena usually didn't sit in the front pew, because she had always wanted to debunk the unofficial, unwritten First Lady code of ethics that outlined in meticulous detail what a pastor's wife must and must not do.

From her perspective, the First Lady's first obligations were to love and serve God, and then her husband, with her whole heart. Where she sat in church and whether she wore a hat or sang in the choir didn't matter much as long as she accomplished the other.

Today, though, she had decided to sit up front for the second time in recent months to let Micah, and everyone who attended this funeral, know she was there with him. John Artis's family filled the center section, so Serena sat in the front pew to the right.

As the somber music swelled and the family filed into the sanctuary in pairs, Serena's eyes welled with tears. She grieved for the mother, already wailing in the front pew, calling out her baby boy's name. Serena grieved for her husband as he prepared to address people for the final time from this pulpit.

Sometimes God seemed so far away, even when you were in his house. Serena knew, though, that he was there. Even when she couldn't feel his presence.

She picked up the bulletin to follow along with the service. Two young ladies who sang with Standing Rock's youth choir came forward and took microphones. In their untrained and unrestrained melodic voices, one soprano, the other alto, they sang "His Eye Is on the Sparrow."

They made it through the second verse before emotions overtook them. Serena, who had often talked to them in their teen group ministry discussions, understood their grief. They had grown up in this neighborhood too and knew John well. Another classmate, another childhood friend, had been snatched by death.

As the girls' mothers helped them to their seats, Micah approached the lectern and looked out into the sea of pain-stricken faces.

The thick silence was filled with tension—Micah's, Serena's, this grieving family's, and that of the spectators who had come to ogle Micah in his final hour as pastor of Standing Rock. Micah stifled it with a simple prayer.

"Lord, be here with this family. Use my words today to honor this young man's life and to honor you."

Micah shared how John had been baptized five months earlier because he was tired of an empty existence.

"John was trying. He wanted to do better in school and do something positive with his life. Trouble was, he couldn't up and leave this neighborhood, his family. The same people who had drawn him to the streets before kept knocking at his door. And when they realized that he wasn't going to come out and play the game anymore, they decided to take him out."

Micah turned to John's family and looked at his mother, whose head was tucked into her chest as she held a handkerchief to her mouth and wept for her only child.

"The drive-by shooters may have ripped John from this earth with their bullets. They may have shot the life out of his body. But they didn't snatch his soul. John professed a love for God. He was secure that his salvation was secure.

"Ms. Artis, please take some comfort in knowing that your child is in heaven, with the God who knew him first."

The congregation affirmed Micah's statements with shouts of "Amen."

He turned his gaze toward the balcony and pointed his finger at the dozens of youths gathered there.

"To those of you up there who think there's nothing more to life than guns, drugs, money, and sex, to those of you who think you might as well live fast and hard now because you doubt you'll make it to your fortieth birthday, to those of you who want to make a change but are afraid it will lead you to wind up like John Artis, I say that today is your day.

"If you came here this morning simply out of respect, simply to say good-bye to this young man, that's all good. But I'm hoping you'll leave here with a new path of your own. It's time to stop playing Russian roulette with your lives, young people. The streets of South Richmond don't have to be the only thing you know about life.

"If you can begin to trust God, he will take you further than you've ever dreamed was possible."

Micah paused.

He stood at the lectern with both arms outstretched and surveyed the crowd.

No one moved.

Then, in the balcony, Serena heard a rustling.

Two girls, trembling and holding hands, left their seats and headed down the aisle. They were followed by five teen boys clad in white T-shirts, blue jeans, and matching blue and white bandanas. Then came an elderly man leaning heavily on a mahogany cane, and a pony-tailed, young girl carrying a tiny baby.

One after the other they came, some in pairs, some stony faced, some in tears.

A mass of people stood at the altar, numbering at least two hundred.

Micah leaned into the microphone and spoke solemnly.

"This is evidence that John's life and death were not in vain."

He turned to the associate ministers, who sat on the pew near Serena.

"We will pray first as a congregation for these tender hearts that stand before us this morning. Then let's pair off with them and pray one-on-one."

The ten ministers in the sanctuary, including Jason Lyons, went to the pulpit and flanked Micah on each side. They clasped each other's shoulders and bowed their heads.

By the time Micah had finished leading the prayer, the congregation was ready to have a Sunday morning worship service.

Bernice, one of the regular Sunday soloists, rose from

her seat in the pews and walked forward to take the microphone next to the piano.

"I grew up with John's mother, Janice, not far from here, in the Stillwell community. When we were young, families tried to stick together; there were some good people there.

"Now to be 'good in the hood' is to give yourself a death sentence," Bernice said. "To want to be better than your surroundings means you're a threat to the people who don't know another way and figure they'll never get out of the ghetto.

"I wasn't here on the Sunday John joined church, but I knew something was different. Every time I saw him in the past few months, there was a sparkle in his eyes. He was on to something, and now I realize what it was.

"So I've come up here today to thank God for saving this young man's life and giving him a new song in his heart. For everyone who has come forward today to try life with God, I want to sing this song in honor of the journey you're embarking on."

Bernice folded one arm across her stomach, closed her eyes, took a deep breath, and with her head thrown back, sang from her soul.

"Lord, I thank you for this day that was not promised to me. Lord, I thank you for my health and strength and saving me one day."

By the time Bernice had finished "Miracles and Blessings," Serena's eyes were swollen from crying. She looked at Micah, who was looking at her too. See what God had done this day, his eyes said to her. No telling what else was in store.

31

So how does it feel to be unemployed?"

Micah's eyes widened at the unexpected question from Bethany, his friend Ian's wife.

"Well . . . ," he began slowly, knowing he couldn't say what was really on his mind. He fiddled with the ribs on his plate, all of a sudden not feeling so hungry.

Music tinkled softly in the background as jazz pianist Debo Dabney caressed the keys on the baby grand positioned on the short stage in a corner of Mister P's.

Serena interrupted.

"Come on, Bethany," she said lightly but with an edge to her voice that Micah suspected wasn't recognized only by him. "You're a stay-at-home mother; you know what it's like to do nothing all day, right?"

Micah squeezed her thigh under the table to silence her. This was going to be a long evening if these two women traded barbs all night. Serena rubbed her husband's hand as it rested on her green linen pants.

In their private language, she was telling him, "I hear ya, babe. I'll chill out. But girlfriend better step back."

Bethany smiled brightly at Serena and ran her fingers through her close-cropped, naturally wavy black hair. If the paparazzi had been nearby, she would have been ready for a photo shoot. Her dark olive complexion, luminous brown eyes, and high-wattage smile, coupled with a size-two Pilates-maintained frame, regularly drew the attention she craved.

"After all, once a beauty queen always a beauty queen," she had told Serena during their initial meeting several years ago. The fact that Serena still remembered the comment and reminded Micah of it every time the four of them made plans to get together told him it still grated on her.

Now that Ian, Bethany, and their daughter, Victoria, had moved to Richmond, Ian called more often to see when they could hang out. Serena begged off as often as she honestly could, but this time there had been no excuse.

Micah's departure from Standing Rock had been publicized by all the local African American publications, with details ranging from the truth—he'd had concerns about Standing Rock pursuing a nationally televised ministry while so much work needed to be done in the community—to the far-fetched—he'd had a vision that he no longer needed to preach and had up and quit the church without giving notice.

Serena had been livid, but Micah had taken it all in stride.

"So this is what it feels like to be a celebrity, huh?" he had said to his wife.

But tonight as he sat at dinner with Ian, Bethany, and Serena, Bethany's question struck him to the core.

He really was out of a job, one he believed God had called him to do. How did he really feel about that?

Before he could muster an answer, Bethany responded to Serena's comments.

"Staying at home by choice is different from doing so due to . . . other circumstances," she said and batted her eyes at Micah sympathetically.

"I know this must be a tough time, but look on the bright side. At least you don't have any children. Worrying about how to take care of them when you're down-and-out would be horrendous."

Ian gave Bethany a look that warned her to shut her mouth. Micah glanced at Serena and saw her eyes cloud over with pain. He had shared their fertility struggles with Ian months ago when Serena had suffered her last miscarriage.

Micah didn't show it as plainly as Serena, but each loss had left wounds on his heart too. Now the wife of one of his best friends was picking at the scar.

Ian squinted his eyes at his wife.

"Let's eat, Bethany," he said between clenched teeth.

Ian turned his head toward his plate and shoved a forkful of collard greens into his mouth.

Bethany shrugged and picked up her utensils to cut the Cobb salad she had ordered.

"Just making conversation, Ian. Settle down. Between being so uptight and that greasy food you're eating, you're going to have a heart attack."

Micah coughed.

"Don't speak destruction over my brother, now," he told her teasingly.

The rest of the evening, Bethany bantered with a sullen Serena about her struggles to find the perfect interior decorator for her new home.

"I mean, the entire six thousand square feet needs to flow one room to the other. What decorators have you used, Serena?"

Micah jumped in before his wife could render another sarcastic reply.

"Serena's so talented that she hasn't needed any additional help. She worked in advertising long enough for her creativity to flow in a variety of arenas. We're just blessed to be in a nice home, sharing it with each other."

Even as he uttered the words, though, his heart sank. He'd been out of work just five weeks, but he knew some changes would have to be made soon.

32

Erika cradled Aaron close to her face and smiled so Charlotte could snap their picture. She cupped his tiny diapered bottom with one hand and his miniature neck with the other.

Jessica, a new shelter resident who also happened to be a hairstylist, had given Erika a cute pixie cut that made her look more striking than usual. Erika's lobes sparkled with the diamond stud earrings D. Haven Interior Designs had given her for helping land the Winchester account.

Her face, now back to its pre-baby thinness, glowed with love for her bundle of joy, who posed perfectly with his fingers intertwined. His little chest moved up and down as he breathed deeply in his sleep.

Charlotte took several more pictures before putting down the camera and taking the baby from Erika's arms. She sat on the sofa, cradling him, and shook her head in disbelief.

"Mmm mmm," Charlotte said and chuckled softly while gently stroking Aaron's jet black, straight hair. "I don't know what this baby's daddy looks like, but he is gorgeous!"

Erika laughed.

"Give me my son. You aren't about to rob this cradle!"

Charlotte turned away as if Erika had actually reached for him.

"You should have gotten all that straight before you asked me to do this job, Miss Thang," Charlotte teased. "You can't take away my 'godmother' title now."

She sat back on the sofa and laid Aaron across her chest, where he seemed to sink into a deeper sleep, if that were possible for a five-week-old.

"Besides, he likes my natural pillows."

"Pillows?" Erika asked.

Charlotte chuckled and gestured toward her size 38C chest.

Erika laughed.

"Oh, those," she said and glanced at her own unusually voluptuous bosom. "I don't know—since I've been nursing, I can hold my own. I want to lose the baby fat, but I'll keep these babies."

Aaron cooed and stirred in Charlotte's arms. Erika's expression grew solemn.

"Just a few more days and I won't be able to hold him," she whispered. She buried her head in her hands.

Charlotte rose slowly so she wouldn't wake the baby and walked over to Erika. She sat next to her and cradled Aaron in one arm so she could take Erika's hand.

"Go ahead and cry if you need to, Erika," Charlotte said. "Giving up your baby, even temporarily, is not an easy thing to do.

"When I moved into this shelter nearly a dozen years ago, I had my four babies with me the whole time. It was extremely hard, but it was the right choice for me at that time. This is the right choice for you and Aaron at this time, and you're sending him somewhere safe, to people you know will love him."

Erika, head bowed, continued to weep in her hands. Charlotte rubbed her back.

"God is working in this situation, Erika. It's no mistake that you need some time to focus on getting established in your new career and getting licensed. Once you do, your world is going to be so different you'll have to work hard to remember you lived in this place.

"And it's no accident that God has arranged for your friend Serena and her husband to take care of Aaron. Whatever work he's doing on that end, Aaron is needed. I know it's hard not to feel guilty, but you are not abandoning your baby.

"Someday you'll tell him all about this and he'll use what the two of you have been through to help somebody else."

Erika leaned her head on Charlotte's shoulder.

"You know, you're more of a mother to me than my biological one. I thank God for hooking us up too."

Charlotte smiled and kissed Aaron's miniature fingers.

"I thank him for everything, Erika, even the things I don't understand."

Erika sat up and looked at her son.

"That's why you're a mama-sized Christian and I'm still crawling."

Charlotte laughed out loud, and Aaron stirred. Erika reached for him, and Charlotte handed him over.

Erika snuggled him close to her face and inhaled his baby scent. At less than two months old, it was too early to tell whom he would eventually resemble, but right now he was a perfect mix between Erika and Elliott, a man he might never see.

Charlotte settled back on the sofa and gazed at mother and son.

"You look like you're playing with your baby brother, not like you just gave birth to him," Charlotte said and smiled.

"Don't make the mistake of thinking that just because people are older than you or have been in church all their lives that they're more saved or more connected to God than you. Going to church and serving on every ministry offered won't save your soul or bring you closer to God.

"Only a sincere effort to know him, to study his Word, and to talk with him can do that. And sometimes the size of your trials matches the size of your faith.

"Joy comes in knowing he's always there no matter what we face. You and Aaron are going to be blessed from this experience."

Erika sighed and prepared to nurse her son. He had started squirming, indicating that he had smelled milk and wanted to eat.

"Thanks, Charlotte. God has shown me through all of this that he's with me no matter what. I don't know how I made it before; I really don't."

Charlotte squeezed her hand.

"It really doesn't matter."

33

Serena stood in the middle of the room and turned all the way around. This was the space she had longed to transform into a nursery, and now it was one.

The three pale blue walls and the sea creatures mural on the fourth wall were stunning. Serena had purchased the mural from an Internet store at a great price and had Micah put it up after he painted. The crib had been donated by a neighbor who had recently moved her third child into a twin-size bed and no longer needed it.

Serena had found a matching dresser and armoire at a local baby store closing sale and had snapped them up.

She strolled over to the armoire and opened one of the drawers. She picked up a pair of the tiny white socks and fingered the edges. Pretty soon precious little feet would be wearing them.

She wished Erika could see where the baby would be staying. The risk of Elliott still staking out the place was too great, though.

Lately he had been ringing the doorbell after midnight.

He would stand on the porch and try to talk to Serena through the door in obviously slurred speech.

His drinking worried Serena, because even though she didn't care for him, she didn't want him to do anything foolish.

Two nights ago he had rung the bell twenty times and had stood there with a bottle of scotch in his hand. Micah had opened the door when Detective Madson arrived, and both men had stood on the porch, with the door ajar, urging Elliott to leave.

Serena had watched and listened to the exchange from the top of the stairs.

"Erika is so selfish," Elliott slurred. "I gave that little twit everything a woman could as' for, and she decides to lea' me. For what? 'Cause I got a bad temper? 'Cause I like my life jus' so? She had everything, man, including a fine husband. I tell you, some women just don' appreciate fine things."

That sent Serena over the edge. She jogged down the stairs and walked onto the porch with her hands on her hips.

"Elliott, before you take your drunk and sorry self home, let me tell you something. You are the worst thing that ever happened to Erika. No man who is really a man has to hit a woman. A real husband wouldn't have beat his wife so much that she felt it necessary to disappear. Maybe if you lay off the booze and stop stalking me, you can get your life together."

Elliott staggered toward Serena.

"Careful, girl," he said slowly. "You're one lick from a coma."

Micah walked over to Elliott and got in his face.

"If I wasn't a man of God, I'd tell you something real special right now, man. You need to get away from my house and get away from my wife."

Detective Madson grabbed Elliott by the forearm and led him toward the squad car in the driveway. He turned to Micah.

"He's in no condition to drive, so I'll take him on home, Reverend. I'm not going to arrest him since he hasn't broken any laws, but I heard what he said to Mrs. McDaniels. I'm noting it in the files."

Detective Madson turned to Elliott and leaned in close. Madson pointed to Serena.

"You come near this woman again, and you're going to jail. No questions asked."

Before Elliott could reply, Micah grabbed Elliott's other arm and helped Detective Madson walk him to the car. Micah turned toward Elliott before Detective Madson opened the rear door for him.

"You know, man, you need to try another way. This anger is eating you up. The booze and whatever else you're taking isn't helping. Prayer is free, and it won't mess up your mind. Whatever you do, though, stay away from my wife."

Elliott laughed.

"Make me, Rev. Micah—oh, that's right. You got fired! Make me, Micah. I know Serena knows something about my wife, and what she knows, I'm going to know, one way or the other."

Detective Madson grabbed the lapel of Elliott's suit.

"That's the second threat of the night. How about we go down to police headquarters instead of to your home?"

Fear filled Elliott's eyes for the first time Serena could recall.

"No, no. I'm a lawyer, man. I can't have a rap sheet. My law firm would lock me out. My career would be over."

Detective Madson looked to Micah for direction on how to proceed. Micah looked at Serena, who shrugged.

"You know what, man, go home and get your life together," Micah said. "Believe it or not, Elliott, I'm going to pray for you."

Serena recalled all of that this afternoon as she searched the top of the dresser for the pictures of the nursery she had prepared for Elliott's child, unbeknownst to him. She had photographed the room and had prints made so Erika would at least have an idea of what the room in which her son would be sleeping looked like.

Serena turned off the light to the nursery and put the photos in her purse. She pushed up the sleeves to her red and white sweat suit and checked her watch.

Tomorrow she and Micah would meet Erika in Old Town Alexandria to exchange information and the baby.

Serena was excited that finally this space would be filled with the noises of infancy she had longed to hear. But just last night she had wet her pillow with tears of sorrow and longing.

Would her child ever sleep in this room? Would she ever have the fulfillment of motherhood? Making that call to cancel the in vitro fertilization procedure still saddled her heart.

Dr. Ritter had been confused.

"I thought you were ready to move forward, Mrs. McDaniels. What changed?"

Serena had sighed and, in a trembling voice, tried to explain.

"Several things have happened, Dr. Ritter. Most importantly, my husband has lost his job. That means the funds we were going to put toward the procedure, coupled with the uncertainty of when we'll have steady income again, means now isn't a good time to bring a baby into the world."

She had wanted to throw up as she said the words.

When is a good time, Lord? Never?

Trust in me and lean not on your own understanding, my child.

Serena heard God, but it didn't make her wait any easier. What if his answer was never? What then? How could she handle this emptiness in her heart?

At least her arms wouldn't be empty. She was going to help Erika by caring for Aaron. And maybe the baby would help her too.

For the first time in recent weeks, she thought about her mother. What would Mama say about how all this was working out—Micah without a job, Erika without a home, Serena longing for a baby, and God sending her one, albeit briefly, through her estranged best friend?

Serena could hear her mother as if she were there in the nursery with her: "God works in mysterious ways, baby, very mysterious ways."

34

By the time night had fallen, Micah knew.

He rose from his knees and gazed at the stars twinkling in the smooth, inky sky. He didn't know where this new call would take him, but for the first time in months, he felt at peace.

As long as you lead the way, God, I'm ready.

He walked from Brown's Island to his car and realized a chill had filled the air. He remembered Serena telling him how she had gone to the nearby Canal Walk in a time of despair. He had come to commune and connect with God, and it had worked.

The quiet, expansive shoreline along the James River had provided the perfect respite for contemplative prayer. In a moment of restlessness, wondering what should be next, where he should go, and what he should do, Micah had driven to the area just south of downtown and parked his car. The restaurants that dotted the walkway along the island had been reopening for dinner, which meant he had had to share the view of the gently lapping water with several young lovers, diners, and people taking an early evening stroll.

Micah had knelt in front of one of the wooden benches, unconcerned about whether his jeans would get dirty or who might see him with his head bowed and hands clasped. When he needed to talk to God, those things didn't matter.

He wasn't sure how long he had stayed in that position, but by the time he had uttered thanks and lifted his head, the temperature had dropped and he had creaky knees.

As he walked to his car now, he thought about what he had realized tonight. It was time to step out on faith and bring to life the ministry God had placed in his heart. He didn't know what resources he would use to do it, where he was going to do it, or who would come, but he had to be obedient.

He opened the door and settled in his seat. He turned the ignition and turned up the volume on his radio, catching the last few seconds of a commercial on 94.1 FM.

"I'm Pastor Jason Lyons. Join us on Sunday nights at eleven o'clock on the Praises Go Up Gospel Network for a Holy Ghost good time! This is an hour of fellowship you just don't want to miss!"

Micah's heart sank. Less than three months after his departure from Standing Rock, he was, for all intents and purposes, old news.

Not in my eyes, son. I love you unconditionally.

He looked in his rearview mirror before backing out but couldn't see much because of the tears blurring his vision.

Was pride making this hurt so much, or was it something else?

Remember your mission. To everything under the sun there is a season. I will never forsake you.

Micah thought about the prayer time he had just had with God, and his heart stopped racing. Maybe Jason was meant to lead Standing Rock in this direction all along. With his natural charisma and good looks, he was definitely photogenic. Micah got his share of compliments, but obviously, God had something else for him to do. That belief had kept him from fighting his firing in court. He might have won, since the congregation had met without his knowledge and voted him out, but God had told him to turn the other cheek, to move on quietly.

He turned off the radio and rode in silence for the rest of the twenty-minute drive home. He and Serena were scheduled to meet Erika in the morning to pick up Aaron. How was he going to tell his wife that not only were they about to begin caring for a newborn, but he was being led to birth a ministry, and it might cost them the few material goods they cherished?

35

Erika gripped the cordless phone until her knuckles glistened. She sat on the sofa in the shelter's family room, clutching a stuffed elephant someone had given her baby.

This might have to be her lifeline for the next few months. Aaron wouldn't miss it. She sniffled and tried to hold the tears at bay as she listened to her boss, Derrick, on the other end of the phone.

He had called this morning to encourage her, as he had been doing since she had given birth six weeks earlier. He had also visited her at the hospital, bringing along a package of diapers for Aaron.

Last week he had treated Erika to lunch while Charlotte watched the baby.

"Do you do this with all of your employees when they have babies?" Erika asked in jest over a lunch of she-crab soup and salmon salad at Georgia Brown's restaurant in northwest Washington, D.C.

Derrick smiled. His square jawline and short haircut gave him a rugged handsomeness that in no way resembled

Elliott's pretty-boy look. Erika was surprised that she found Derrick attractive. He wasn't her usual type. But then again, she was surprised to be thinking along those lines anyway. He was her boss—they weren't on a date. At least Derrick hadn't said so, and besides, she was still married.

He took her hand in his after lunch and offered to pray with her.

Erika was startled, but she could see the sincerity in his eyes. After all, hadn't she met him while he was volunteering at Goodwill?

"I'd be honored, Derrick," she said softly. "I'm new to this faith thing, so I'm a little nervous about praying in public, but as long as you're okay, I'll hang."

Derrick looked around and shrugged, his tailored black jacket settling easily onto his shoulders.

"I don't like PDP much either, but today is a good time to make an exception."

Erika, whose hand still rested in his, frowned.

"PDP? That's a new one on me."

"Public displays of prayer, you know, like PDA—public displays of affection," he had chuckled lightly, his husky voice growing huskier. "Don't tell anybody how corny I am. Especially our clients."

They ended the lunch with him offering a brief prayer that God would keep Erika and Aaron safe and give Erika the strength to let her son go for a while so she would be better prepared in the long run to care for him.

Today his phone call was just as reassuring as his presence had been that afternoon.

"I haven't told you that my mother was once in your shoes," Derrick said while Erika, still clutching the stuffed animal, leaned back into the dingy sofa and closed her eyes.

"What?"

"My mother got pregnant with me when she was a sophomore in college. My grandparents were insistent that she complete her education, so they raised me while she studied for both her undergraduate and graduate degrees.

"I lived with them in Missouri until I was about six years old."

"Really?"

"Really. And I love them dearly to this day."

"How do you feel about your mom?"

"We have a very close relationship. She went on to get her doctorate in psychology and now teaches at Penn State.

"When I was a little boy, I thought it was normal that I lived with my gran and grandad and saw my mom only a couple of times a month. I was already school age when she was finally ready to take care of me, so that was an adjustment. But your son will still be so young; I'm sure it will be an easier transition."

Erika's spirits brightened. She wasn't the only person in the world going through something like this. In her head she had known that all along, but to talk to someone who had personally lived through such an experience was reassuring.

She almost spoke but changed her mind.

Derrick picked up on the hesitation.

"What is it?"

"Why are you being so nice to me, Derrick? Why do you care so much?"

"There's nothing wrong with helping each other, Erika. Friends do that. All of us at D. Haven want to help you get through this period and get you prepared for life as an interior designer. If there's ever more to my story, you'll be the first to know."

36

The wind howled, and the rain lashed at the windows with a scary fury. Serena wondered if it was a sign. Was God crying with Erika today, knowing her heart would be heavy?

They had decided to meet in Old Town Alexandria so Erika wouldn't have to drive any closer to Richmond and risk Elliott seeing her. With all the rain, Serena had worried that they should change the location.

Charlotte had taken the phone from Erika to reassure Serena.

"Don't worry, dear. Babies don't melt in the rain. Today's the day. We need to do this so Erika can get refocused on her mission."

Serena initially had considered Charlotte callous. But the more she thought about it, she realized the woman was right. Prolonging Erika's separation from Aaron would only make things harder.

Serena sighed as they approached the King Street exit

that would take them into Old Town. Her stomach was turning flips. She had longed for a baby for years, but now that one was about to be placed in her arms, what on earth was she going to do with him?

If only Mama were here.

She was blessed, though, to have a mother-in-law who considered both Serena and Micah her children. Mrs. Mc-Daniels was scheduled to fly in on Tuesday and stay for a week to help with Aaron. But that was four days away. Would they survive until then?

Serena voiced her concerns to her husband again, and yet again Micah reminded her how well prepared they were.

"The crib's in place, we've got diapers and formula, and you have the next three weeks off work," Micah said. "Stop worrying, love. Just picture Aaron sleeping and playing in that nursery you've created."

She noticed that Micah had been quiet the past few days, though, prompting her to wonder if he were having second thoughts about taking Aaron. Caring for the baby was going to be more expensive than they had initially considered.

Footing the bill for the formula, diapers, clothing, and car seats had led them to dip heavily into their savings. When Serena went back to work and Micah landed a job, they would be adding child-care costs to the budget too, and Erika was in no position to contribute financially.

In the meantime Micah had signed up to serve as a substitute teacher for Richmond Public Schools.

"This will keep me busy and give me a little pocket

change while I'm praying and pondering over what's next, love," he had said.

Serena knew this was a difficult time for him, especially now that the Standing Rock services were airing on PGU every week and it was all the talk of Richmond.

Even Serena's nosy Aunt Flora had called to inquire about Micah's reaction.

"You think he's sorry he left, Serena? Was he afraid of TV or something? He's not running from the law, is he? You know how when people get on national TV their skeletons start coming out. Does he have some big secret?"

It had taken everything within Serena not to hang up on Herman Jasper's baby sister. If Aunt Flora ever learned the truth about Serena's heritage, that she was actually the daughter of Melvin Gates, she might not bother calling again.

Serena had considered blurting it out: "Aunt Flora, don't worry about Micah. My real daddy—you know, Melvin Gates—he's made sure that my husband is on the up and up."

Serena envisioned that scenario but knew she would never do it.

Today, though, as they got closer and closer to the cobblestone streets and historic buildings in Alexandria, doubt about everything she had once clung to was surfacing.

Micah was too quiet. The funds were getting low. She had no idea what to do with a baby.

Peace be still, my daughter. I am with you.

That still, small voice always soothed her.

They pulled into a parking lot on South Washington Street, adjacent to the city's history museum, and Micah and Serena searched for the blue van that belonged to Naomi's Nest. As they cruised through the lot, the rain abated.

Serena peered through the windshield at the suddenly sunny sky and, off to her left, saw a faint rainbow.

God had sent her a rainbow when he took Mama to heaven. She heard him loud and clear today.

Micah turned down another row and saw a van meeting the description Erika had given them. He pulled his Jeep alongside it and peered into the passenger window.

Serena leaned around him and looked too. She saw Erika holding her baby close to her, peppering his soft face with kisses. Tears filled Serena's eyes.

She hadn't seen her friend in almost five years, but she still loved Erika like a sister. She could see the pain in Erika's eyes, and it pierced her heart. In her own way, she understood what Erika probably couldn't articulate.

Serena couldn't have a baby and grieved for the barrenness of her womb. Erika had given birth to another life and was grieving to release him so soon.

Serena climbed out of the Jeep and walked over to the passenger side of the van. Erika passed the baby to Charlotte, who sat in the driver's seat, then bowed her head in her hands and wept.

Serena opened the door, leaned into the van, and wrapped her arms around her friend's petite shoulders. The years and issues that had separated them fell away like bitter memories.

Today, and really for the rest of Aaron's life, they would be united in a common cause, no matter who raised him.

"I'm here, E. It's going to be okay."

Erika embraced Serena and whispered fiercely, "Please love my baby. Please let him know how much I love him. He's all I have, Serena. He's all I have."

Serena squeezed her harder.

"You have more than you think, Erika. Everything is going to be fine."

37

The giggles coming from the bathroom lured Micah again.

Every night, just as he prepared to settle into his favorite spot on the sofa and spend some time zoning out with TV or a *Motor Trend* magazine, the laughter and baby gibberish distracted him.

Serena doesn't need my help, he'd tell himself. *I better take this quiet time while I can.*

Before he knew it, though, he'd find himself sitting on the edge of the tub, playing with the colorful rings on the bath seat Aaron sat in or squeezing water from a squeaky duck the color of sunshine into the cheeky boy's face.

Sometimes Micah came close to referring to himself as Daddy when he spoke to the toothless six-month-old with Erika's grin and gray-green eyes. Then he'd check himself and ask God to help him to be patient for his own son.

Aaron was easy to fall in love with. Micah and Serena couldn't have asked for a better baby.

"What if our own child is a little terror?" Serena said in

jest tonight, indicating to Micah that she hadn't stopped praying to get pregnant.

Aaron gurgled with giggles as she rubbed liquid baby soap over his chest and abdomen and tickled him in the process. "Wouldn't that be something? We have Erika's son, a little angel, and then our child comes along and gives us a run for our money."

Micah's laugh sounded hollow to his own ears.

Serena squeezed warm water from the washcloth over Aaron's back and cast a questioning glance at Micah.

"What's up?" she asked.

Micah grabbed the hooded towel from a bench near the tub and extended his arms toward Aaron. Serena put the baby in Micah's arms so he could dry him off and slather him with lotion.

She sat back on her heels and watched.

Micah finally answered.

"A lot. We have to talk."

He had wanted to tell her for a while now about the vision God had laid on his heart, but he knew it could turn their world upside down—more than it already was.

Serena took Aaron from Micah and quickly diapered him before he could wiggle free. She squeezed the infant's sumo wrestler thighs into a one-piece velour sleeper.

She kissed his cheeks until he gave her another broad, gummy grin.

"This one is for your mommy," Serena said and chewed on his left cheek with her lips. "And this one is from me, Auntie Ree."

Aaron jammed his fingers in his mouth, all the while smiling.

Serena rose from the floor with the baby and looked at Micah.

"I'm ready to listen. Let's put the baby to sleep first."

Micah put away the bath supplies and joined Serena in the nursery. She had dimmed the lights and was sitting in a rocker, humming softly to a quickly fading Aaron.

Micah stood in the doorway, watching her, falling in love with her all over again. If she could love someone else's baby this much, he couldn't imagine how she would open her heart for her own.

Before his mother had returned to Oklahoma after helping out with Aaron for a week, she had told her son that for Serena it probably would be pretty much the same.

"Don't you see, son? She loves Aaron as if he were hers. She hasn't compartmentalized her love and put him in the 'temporary stay' category. It's going to be hard for her when she has to give the baby back to Erika, but I tell you, it is a beautiful thing to see."

Micah had agreed with his mother then, and he did so again tonight.

Serena laid Aaron in his crib and turned on the musical mobile attached to the side to help soothe him to sleep. She and Micah would rock him for a while but never let him fall all the way asleep in their arms, at his mother's suggestion.

"Let him be sleepy enough to want to go all the way but awake enough that he realizes he's going to sleep on his own," Mrs. McDaniels had advised. It had been working.

Serena tiptoed over to the dresser and turned on the baby monitor so they could hear Aaron if he cried. She left the door open just a crack and joined Micah in the hallway. He put his arm around her shoulders and led her to his study.

She raised an eyebrow.

"You're taking me to the office? This must be serious."

Micah didn't reply. It was serious, and he had pondered for the longest how to tell her. Now that the time had come, he didn't want to make too much small talk.

Knowing Serena, he probably didn't have anything to worry about. But this was a plan he couldn't carry out on his own. Giving birth to his dream might further delay hers.

38

By the time Micah had turned on a lamp and had joined her on the futon in his office, Serena's palms were sweating. Just what did he have to tell her?

He had been quiet lately, but she attributed that to the stress and uncertainty of no longer pastoring Standing Rock and the way in which he had been removed. She had thought he might not be enjoying his substitute teaching gig or maybe even wondering when she was ever going to get pregnant. Even with all the turmoil, they hadn't stopped trying.

Tonight she realized that whatever had been keeping Micah so pensive wasn't so simple.

He sat next to her and took her hands in his. He locked eyes with her and kissed her lips.

"Don't look so scared, love. It's not that bad."

Serena's expression softened, but she didn't speak, indicating that she wanted him to go on.

"I know you've been praying for me to find out my next step and what God wants me to do. Well, he has told me, loud and clear.

"It's no surprise to you that I've been troubled by the murders and youth violence in the city for a long time. That's one of the reasons I wanted Standing Rock members to focus more on community outreach. We've got to stop just talking about God's goodness and start showing it to people who are hurting and hating and killing. We've got to reach out to the kids before they get sucked into that generational cycle of violence, drugs, and apathy."

Micah rose and paced the floor in front of Serena.

"God wants me to start a ministry in Stillwell, in the heart of the violence, so we can reach those kids and their parents and grandparents."

Serena sat on the edge of the sofa and looked up at her husband.

"Are you saying you want to start a church?"

"Yes and no."

Micah sat next to her again.

"It would be a place of worship, of course, but it won't be your traditional church with Sunday services and Bible study and a few ministries here and there. We'll still have all of that, mind you, but the true focus will be meeting people's needs. Feeding them if they're hungry, crying with them and praying for them if they're hurting, sometimes just listening and offering sound advice lifted from the pages of the Bible. You get it?"

Serena nodded slowly.

"I get the mission," she said. "I see what you want to accomplish, but how? Where would the church hold services and other meetings? Where would the people come from?"

Micah smiled.

"Technical questions, love. I asked them too. God has told me to let him worry about the details. All I know is that it will likely be donated space in a community center format. When we begin to give away food and meet people at their point of need without judging them, believe me, they'll come. They'll crave to know Jesus's unselfish, unconditional love."

"I understand the heart behind this effort, Micah, but the technical questions are important too," Serena said solemnly.

He nodded and took her hand again.

"I know, love. I know. And I really am trusting God to provide us with a place. But here's the hard part: whatever we do, even if we have others willing to join with us by donating food, volunteering their time, or helping in other ways, we're going to have to put up some of our own money. We're going to have to foot the bill for a lot of things to get this ministry afloat, from buying food to give away to paying the electricity bill when we do get a place.

"It means," he looked at her pensively, "that some other things might have to temporarily wait."

He waited for a response, but Serena was silent.

"I'm not saying wait forever, but we're quickly depleting our savings caring for Aaron, paying the mortgage on this house, and covering other expenses. My substitute teaching income barely pays for diapers, and you can't sustain us forever on your nonprofit salary."

Serena thought she knew where he was going with this—the fifty thousand dollars Melvin Gates had offered her.

Her heart sank. Then she looked into Micah's eyes and saw the sorrow and uncertainty pooled there. He wanted a family too, but right now it was more important to be obedient.

Serena took his hand in hers and squeezed it.

"I'm with you, Micah McDaniels, wherever God leads. The fifty thousand dollars is yours for the ministry. And if we need to sell this house and move back into Mama's house in North Side to live free of charge, we can do that. The couple who have been renting plan to move out next month when they close on their first home. I can turn my old bedroom into a little boy's blue haven for Aaron."

Serena understood now why she had never been willing to sell Mama's house after her death. She had chalked it up to sentimental reasons and the fact that someday she would want to show her children where she had grown up. Micah would keep the grass cut, and she would go by occasionally to dust and sit with her memories.

Now, years after Mama's passing, she was thankful she had been so hesitant to let the property go.

Maybe the adage that one could never go home again wasn't always true. She was going, this time with her husband and her best friend's baby, but it was still home. Mama's spirit would be there to guide her.

Micah cupped Serena's face with both his hands and put his forehead to hers.

"I love you, Serena Jasper McDaniels. You are a beautiful person."

"Ditto, babe."

39

Erika strolled down Aisle Three for the third time and stood in front of Elmo. She couldn't decide whether to buy cups, plates, and other paraphernalia bearing the ticklish red monster's image or that of Thomas the Tank Engine. One-year-olds didn't know or care much anyway, but her baby was going to have a special first birthday party.

She was thriving in her interior design career and loved it. Derrick had indicated that in another year, after she received her interior design certificate from a local university, she would probably be ready to take the National Council for Interior Design exam, which she needed in order to obtain a state license.

Aaron was healthy, happy, and handsome. Somehow Serena had taught him to call Erika Mommy. He knew her voice and said Mommy every time she called and when she occasionally risked a visit. It had been too difficult to go long periods without seeing her son. Serena had taken pictures of Erika every time she visited and hung them on the walls in Aaron's room so he would know who she was.

Sometimes Charlotte would drive her down to Richmond, and sometimes after work Derrick would offer to take her. He and Micah would hang out or play a round of golf while she visited with the baby and Serena.

Derrick had shared some great news with her last night that she couldn't wait to announce when she visited this weekend.

Erika knew Serena was busy on her end too, ordering a special cake for Aaron from Westhampton Bakery and inviting children from the home-based day care he attended to a party at the Children's Museum of Richmond. The executive director of the museum was a colleague of Serena's and had given Serena an opportunity to host Aaron's party there as a gift to the birthday boy.

Mrs. Brown, the retired teacher and former member of Standing Rock who cared for Aaron and three other toddlers in her home, had offered to provide pizza. Aaron went to her house three and a half days a week and loved his "big boy school."

Aaron and his guests likely wouldn't understand the big to-do with the cake and candles, but they would love visiting the various sections of the museum, from the mock grocery store to the art room to the winding jungle tunnel.

Erika could envision the joy on her son's face. She knew that the sacrifices Serena and Micah were making, and the attentiveness of Mrs. Brown, were helping put it there.

It had been hard for Erika to trust anyone other than Serena for a long time. When Erika had arrived at Naomi's

Nest, Charlotte's love and attention had begun to crack the glacier around her heart. Whenever she snuck into Richmond and saw the unconditional love this stranger, Mrs. Brown, gave her son, it raised her hopes that there were more good people in the world than there were mean-spirited ones, like Elliott.

Erika had been stunned when Serena informed her that she and Micah were leaving their spacious new house to return to Serena's childhood home in North Side. They had reassured her that no matter what, they would still take care of Aaron, but she had worried whether the change in Micah's job status and their relocation would be too much with a baby involved. Serena had also adjusted her professional life and received permission from the board of directors of the Children's Art Coalition to work a four-day week, which included a telecommute arrangement on the fourth day.

Erika's fears had been unwarranted. Serena and Micah had rolled with the punches as if Aaron were their own. When they had relocated, Serena gave Aaron the room she had once cherished. Erika felt safer coming to visit them now because she knew Elliott didn't frequent North Richmond unless he had a specific purpose.

Her midafternoon reverie was broken when a Party Central cashier wandered over to her and smiled.

"Need some help finding something, ma'am?"

Erika shook her head and reached for the Elmo items.

"No thanks. I've finally decided," Erika told her. "Elmo it is. We're going to party like never before."

40

Micah pushed open the door to Sheridan's Barbershop and looked at the men and boys waiting to get their hair cut.

With every seat taken, the shop resembled a standing-room-only Sunday morning worship service, especially with it being the day before Easter. The brothers were shooting the breeze, and the barbers were cutting hair and talking smack.

Micah glanced at his watch. It was ten o'clock, and Aaron's party started at two thirty.

His barber, Nick, nodded at him.

"What's up, man. Wait's at least an hour."

Micah grabbed a copy of *Sports Illustrated* and took a seat at the end of the row, near the door.

"That'll work, man," he said.

Micah flipped several pages in the magazine before realizing a silence had descended over the shop.

He looked up, and it hit him.

"What? Ya'll can't talk now that a preacher's in the

house? Come on, now. It don't have to be like that. Tell 'em, Nick. None of them will show up in my next sermon."

Laughter broke the tension, and the various conversations resumed.

Nick shook his head and kept trimming the hair of the boy who sat patiently in his chair as the boy's father stood next to him and watched.

"You're all right with me, Rev," Nick said.

Micah opened the magazine again and was about to delve into the cover article when the guy next to him struck up a conversation.

"I hear you've started a church, Rev. McDaniels. How's that going?"

Micah didn't know the man but realized he had probably read a story or announcement in the local African American community newspapers about Micah inviting people to fellowship on Saturdays and Sundays in a nontraditional worship setting. Micah had used his status as a substitute teacher to obtain permission from the school superintendent to hold weekend services in the gym at Stillwell Elementary School. He and Serena used some of the proceeds from the sale of their house to pay a stipend for utilities, but there was no rental fee. After much prayer Micah had settled on the name New Hope Community Ministries.

He had worn jeans and a white collared long-sleeve shirt when the first service had been held three months ago. Serena and Aaron had been dressed the same.

That first Saturday four people came, including an elderly woman who was raising the ten-year-old granddaughter she brought with her, a homeless man who likely wanted shelter from the afternoon rainstorm, and a pregnant girl who looked as if she was no more than thirteen. Serena had seen the girl a day earlier in the Food Mart on the corner and had given her a flyer with details about the service.

Micah asked them to form a small circle with the folding chairs that he and Serena had purchased from a flea market sale. As Serena held a bouncing Aaron, Micah prayed for the people in the circle.

Then, rather than standing in front of them, he sat there with his Bible and shared a simple message about how God loved them no matter what and how that would be the mission of New Hope Community Ministries as well.

"He can use and redeem anyone," Micah told them that day. "God is not a respecter of persons. He doesn't consider one person better than another. That's right here in the Bible. Regardless of what you've done or what you've been told, you are still God's child, and he wants to live in your heart."

The small group ate a meal of cold-cut sandwiches, chips, and punch. Serena had made a yellow sheet cake in honor of the first service.

The next day those four returned, and five others joined them. Micah spent the rest of that week canvassing the neighborhood, talking to the steely-eyed teenagers on the corners, the older residents who were wary about leaving their homes for fear that someone would rob them while they were gone, and the young girls who had decided to secure unconditional love by having babies and leaving school.

The following week's Saturday service included twenty

people. Micah held a pair of sneakers in the air by the shoe-laces and looked into the eyes of each person present.

"These look like nothing more than a pair of worn shoes, but they represent a life. Last night I visited the mother of Marco Andrews. He was wearing black high tops when he was gunned down in the East End on Wednesday, but these shoes were among the many pairs lining the shelf in his closet.

"Marco Andrews cared about these shoes. He did what-ever he had to do to get them. Police say he was killed for failing to hand over all the money to his higher-ups in the drug ring he was part of. They shot him in the head twice and left him to die in front of an elementary school where two second graders found his body the next morning."

Micah paused. There were no gasps. This was a shell-shocked community used to hearing stories like this.

Only Serena sat there incredulous. Micah knew that each time she heard a sad ending to a life like this one, it rattled her. He knew that as she sat there with her eyes closed, rocking a sleepy Aaron while he rested his head on her chest, she was praying that the ears and hearts of those present would be open to God's message.

Those humble beginnings flashed through Micah's mind today as he prepared to answer the man's question about how the ministry was going. It wasn't something he rated based on attendance and offerings. That's why he and his wife had sacrificed so much to have the funds they would need.

Micah smiled and shrugged.

"Just to have the doors open and one or two people com-ing in means it's going well. It's not about the numbers. It's really about changing the hearts of people who have been so beaten down that they think there's no other way to live than the violence and death they've been surrounded by for so long," Micah said. "We just want to give them hope that there's another way, a better way, and it's theirs for the taking. You should come visit sometime. I'm sure you have a lot to offer to the young boys who need strong male role models."

The man seemed surprised by Micah's candidness.

"A preacher who doesn't care about the numbers? You're the first one I've met."

Micah shrugged.

"We're out there, man. Don't let the problems in the church keep you from taking time to be with God. There are problems everywhere. You still go to work, don't you? You still spend time with your family, and all of us have dysfunction. Your reasons for going to church will determine what you get out of it.

"We need money at New Hope, just like everyone else. But more than that, we need to reach out to people and serve them first. The rest will come."

The man's eyes filled with respect.

As the door to the barbershop swung open again, the man shook Micah's hand.

"You're all right, Rev. McDaniels. Don't be surprised if you see me there one Saturday or Sunday."

Micah patted his back.

"Come as you are, man. No pomp and circumstance is needed, just a willingness to help out in the community."

Micah leaned back in his seat and looked up to see Elliott standing in front of him.

"Well, well, well. If it isn't Mr. Preacher Man," Elliott
sneered. "You come over here to get your hair cut too,
huh?"

Micah looked at his magazine and then back at Elliott.

"I've been coming for years, Elliott. What brings you
over to Jackson Ward? This isn't your usual place to be
seen, is it?"

"Since my wife has gone missing, I hang out wherever I
can. You just never know when you might spot her. Even
preachers can be sneaky. I know you know something,
Micah McDaniels. You're trying to be a saint, but you don't
keep a man from his wife."

Elliott had begun to raise his voice, and the shop fell
silent again.

Nick put down his clippers and looked at Elliott.

"Hey, bruh, we don't do that in here. You need to take
that outside."

Elliott's eyes flashed. He was about to say something
that Micah could sense he might end up regretting. Micah
rose from his seat and steered Elliott toward the door. He
looked back at Nick.

"Hold my spot. I'll be back in a minute."

Micah walked toward the side of the building with Elliott following him.

When they had reached a spot outside the view of
everyone in the shop, Micah turned to Elliott.

"Did you come in that shop because you saw my car
parked outside? As much as you stalk me and my wife, I
know you know what I drive."

Elliott squinted his eyes and put his face close to Micah's.

"What if I did? You need to let me know where my wife is. It's been almost two years since she left, but she's still my wife. If I ever get my hands on her, I'll—"

Micah put his finger in Elliott's face and spoke through clenched teeth.

"That's exactly why you don't know where she is, Elliott. You're a wife beater. You don't deserve her if all you can do is slap her around."

Elliott seemed taken aback by Micah's fervor. All the time Micah had spent with Erika and Aaron over the past year had made him protective of them. He knew Erika's heart. She would have loved to have a happy, intact family. But thank God she had wised up and realized that what appeared to be picture perfect often had nothing to do with reality.

Micah's anger deflated as he looked into Elliott's pitiful eyes.

"Look, Elliott. This has been going on for too long. If I could tell you something about Erika and trust that you wouldn't harm her, I would have done so by now. What you need to understand is that at this point, it's really not about Erika. She has been gone for a long time, and you've been trying to keep up the farce that your marriage is still okay.

"This is about you getting you straight, man. You have to find out what's going on inside you that keeps you so angry, that made you beat your wife instead of taking care of her. What keeps you stalking me and my wife instead of trying to heal your wounds."

Elliott frowned.

"Don't be preaching to me out here on the street. If I want to hear a sermon, there's a church on just about every corner."

Micah nodded.

"Yep. And you've passed by them many times. It's not about the church anyway, Elliott. God can fill your heart anywhere, anytime, man. It's about you wanting him to.

"I've got to get back in the shop, but you know what? I'm still praying for you, Elliott. Everybody needs it, even when they don't realize it."

Elliott stood there expressionless. Micah turned and walked back toward Sheridan's.

Thank God he had decided not to bring Aaron with him to the barbershop today. One good look at the boy and Elliott would have seen the resemblance to himself and to Erika.

41

Erika watched from the doorway as Serena changed the roll of film for the second time and squatted as ladylike as she could in her ivory skirt.

"Say 'Happy Easter,' Aaron!" she said and snapped a picture of his toothy, bright-eyed grin.

He looked adorable in his navy jacket and white tailored shorts with matching knee-high socks and white hard-soled shoes. He held a powder blue basket filled with eggs and jelly beans in one hand and a blue bunny in the other.

"How many pictures are you going to snap, love?"

Serena turned to Micah and laughed. "I guess I'll keep going until I don't have any film left."

Erika strolled into the room, and smiled. She was dressed in white linen, her auburn hair perfectly coifed in the pixie cut she still wore. She looked like an angel, and for the first time in a long time, she felt happy too.

Sometimes she felt like an intruder on Serena, Micah, and Aaron, but Serena often reminded her that was unwarranted. Serena and Micah did their best to let her know that this was her family too and that she was indeed Aaron's mother.

Serena extended the camera toward Erika.

"Want to take some pictures of your baby?"

Erika laughed.

"That's okay. Looks like you've already done a studio shoot."

Serena shrugged and smiled sheepishly.

"These are precious moments. Better yet, why don't you go over there with Aaron and I'll get both of you in the shots."

They wound up going out to the backyard. Serena positioned them near the magnolia tree her mother had loved and snapped six photos. She promised to get at least one of them enlarged and framed for Erika to put on her desk at work.

The doorbell rang as they went back inside.

"That's probably Charlotte," Erika said and strode toward the front door. She had invited her friend and mentor to join her at Micah's new church for Easter.

Charlotte had agreed to drive down for the service and for Easter dinner. Since Erika hadn't saved enough money yet to purchase a car, Charlotte would also take her back to northern Virginia, where she had recently rented an apartment with another former Naomi's Nest resident.

Erika opened the door and hugged Charlotte, who was wearing a pink coatdress and matching pumps. For the first time in the twenty-one months Erika had known her, Charlotte was wearing her usually braided hair loose.

Thick silver and black curls framed her lovely face, which was enhanced with eye shadow, blush, and lipstick.

"You look marvelous, Charlotte!"

Charlotte kissed her cheeks.

"Happy Easter, sweetie. I knew I was coming down here with the divas, so I figured I'd do it up nicely. You look lovely too."

She extended a bouquet of flowers toward Erika.

"Your boss asked me to deliver these."

Erika blushed and took the colorful bouquet Derrick had sent. She read the card as Charlotte stepped inside.

"I know he likes you, and you seem to like him too. Just take it slow, Erika. God will tell you when, and if, the time is right. You've still got a lot of healing to do."

Erika nodded as she closed the door.

"I agree, and so does Derrick. We've talked about it."

She showed Charlotte the note Derrick had put on the card.

Erika, I know big changes are in store for you. I am happy to walk with you on the journey, as a friend. Happy Easter. May the rebirth that this special season represents be meaningful to you in more ways than one. bless ya, Derrick

Charlotte smiled and squeezed her hand.

"Where's that little boy of mine?"

Erika laughed.

"Forgive me for being so rude. Let's go find him. Serena has been taking pictures all morning. I'm sure she'll want to get you in a few shots too."

Aaron was in his room, sitting on his bed while Serena tied his shoes for the tenth time that morning.

"How's my little man doing?" Charlotte asked as she knelt beside the bed. "I'm sorry I missed your party yesterday. Aunt Charlotte had to work. How was it? How does it feel to be one year old?"

Aaron answered with a giggle.

"You should have seen his face when we put a piece of cake in front of him and let him go for it," Erika said. "He needed a bath by the time he waded through it. More of it ended up on his face than in his mouth!"

Micah and Serena grabbed their belongings and headed for the door. Erika, Charlotte, and Aaron followed them outside to the driveway.

Micah removed Aaron's car seat from his Jeep and passed it to Charlotte, who had become a pro at buckling it into the rear seat of her Honda.

They arrived at New Hope Community Ministries and found the school parking lot filled with cars.

They entered through a rear door that led into what Micah had dubbed the ministry's recreation space. The six adolescent girls who participated in a fledgling praise dance ministry were rehearsing their routine for the morning service.

"Left, two, three, four. Right, two, three, four."

Kira, the group's director and a former professional dancer, intently led the girls through the moves with the focus of a skilled surgeon.

Micah slipped away into a small side office he used as a study. Serena led Erika, Charlotte, and the baby into the gym, which served as the sanctuary. They slid into the third row of folding chairs, next to Tawana's mother.

Serena was thrilled to see Ms. Carter.

"I'm so glad you made it!" She leaned past Ms. Carter and gave her goddaughter Misha a kiss. "You look so pretty! Did you enjoy Aaron's party yesterday?"

Misha nodded shyly. She was wearing the shimmery lavender and green dress Serena had given her for Easter, with a white shawl draped around her shoulders. Her sandy brown hair curled past her shoulders and was secured by a lavender headband. When she smiled, her deep dimples left commas in her cheeks.

"Is your mom singing today?"

Misha nodded again. She looked past Serena and waved at Aaron, who scrambled from Erika's lap and toddled past Ms. Carter to grab Misha's hands.

Erika laughed.

"I'm losing him to another woman already," she whispered in Serena's ear.

Serena laughed, but her heart clenched. She felt the same way about what she knew was likely to happen soon—having to return Aaron to Erika.

The service began with Tawana singing a stirring version of "The Old Rugged Cross."

Erika hung her head and let the tears fall without shame. Serena put her arms around her friend's shoulders and squeezed her tight. She was so thankful that Erika finally knew there was a God and that he was a friend and much, much more.

Micah, who still didn't use a lectern or have a formal altar, stood in the center of a semicircle of folding chairs that extended six rows back. He still tended to dress casually, but today he had opted for the traditional suit and tie. Instead of black, navy, or tan, he wore white.

"I don't typically stand before you dressed like a preacher," Micah said to a roar of laughter. "But since I happen to be one, and this happens to be a glorious day in our faith, I wanted to do something to make it memorable and to honor our Savior's sacrifice.

"White is symbolic of purity and wholeness, but I come today submitting that it also exemplifies rebirth, or a period of starting over.

"Easter, in the pagan sense of the celebration, focuses on the rebirth or return of spring, and as a byproduct, the rebirth or renewal of hope. In our faith it deals with the resurrection of Christ.

"For those of us here at New Hope Community Ministries, all of the above apply. Some of us are struggling with guilt or shame over things that happened long ago, things that can't be changed, or things that, in the long run, have nothing to do with who we are and how we're loved by God. It's those things that we must release so that we can be renewed.

"Some of us have so many skeletons in our closets that the doors won't close."

Micah had to laugh at the chorus of "Amens" and the hands that reached heavenward in affirmation.

"The celebration of Easter is our annual commemoration of Jesus's death and resurrection on our behalf. Yet it's also a reminder that we have an opportunity, through our faith, to start anew.

"It doesn't mean you have to become a saint, because Lord knows I'm not. It doesn't mean you have to be holier than thou, because God hates a show-off. All it means is that your heart is seeking God. You want to know him better and love like he loves. Instead of complicating your life, it makes things so much simpler."

By the time Micah was finished, about a dozen of the sixty or so people in the room had come forward for prayer or to join the church.

Serena was startled to see a tearful Elliott standing on the fringe of the crowd, his head bowed and his lips silently moving. She nudged Erika, whose eyes bulged when she saw her estranged husband for the first time since the night of their fourth wedding anniversary. She glanced down at Aaron, who was sleeping in her arms, and passed him to Serena.

"You want to leave while he's not looking?" Serena asked.

Erika started to agree but hesitated. She leaned over to whisper in Serena's ear.

"I'm not running from him anymore, Serena. I've got to face him sometime, and today must be that day."

Erika sat back in her chair and folded her arms. She sang along softly with the four teenagers who stood behind Micah with microphones, belting out the lyrics to Hezekiah Walker's "Second Chance."

As they sang "You're the God of a second chance," Elliott approached Micah and offered to shake his hand. Micah grabbed him and gave him a hug instead. The two men spoke softly for a few minutes and turned toward the worshipers.

"I've known this man standing here next to me for a while now," Micah said. "He told me I could share with you what he came up here for, because he's ready to make a change."

Erika and Serena exchanged glances. Charlotte looked at them curiously. Erika leaned over and explained that Elliott was her husband. Charlotte sat up straighter to listen.

"I could tell you what he said," Micah continued, "but you need to hear it from him. He needs to say the words out loud."

Serena watched pensively. She wondered if Micah was nudging Elliott to speak for himself because Erika was there and would hear his remorse, admission of guilt, or whatever he had to say.

Elliott's hand shook as he took the microphone from Micah. Tears still streamed from his eyes as Micah stood next to him and clapped his shoulder with his massive hand.

"Take your time."

Elliott scanned the faces of the people in front of him. Serena thanked God that Erika was so petite; Elliott probably hadn't seen her sitting behind the woman with the flower-laden green straw hat.

He cleared his throat.

"For as long as I can remember, I've been angry with the world. I've put up a front that I'm all this and all that—at work, at home, and in between. But in my dreams the real me comes out. That boy, that man, is afraid of not fitting in because of secrets in my house that nobody knows about.

"I never invited friends from school over because I never knew when my father would pick a fight with my mother. And I stayed angry with my mother for never standing up to him. When she did finally leave him, after he shot her five times and left her walking with a limp, I was furious with her for disrupting our family.

"I've never measured up in either of my parents' eyes." Elliott laughed bitterly.

"My mother was proud when I got my law degree—in fact, she worked extra hours to put me through law school. But then she began immediately riding me about making partner so I could pay her back. And my father, who has never found a decent job since serving time for shooting my mother, wants to know why I'm not a judge yet.

"The sad thing is that I became just like him," Elliott said. "I had a beautiful wife who ran away in the middle of the night almost two years ago because I had a habit of showing my love by beating her."

Charlotte reached for Erika's hand and gave her a comforting squeeze. Serena, who held the sleeping Aaron, found a tissue in her purse and passed it to the weeping Erika.

"The night she left me was our wedding anniversary. How had I celebrated it? By coming in from work and giving her a black eye."

Some of the ladies in the congregation who had seen or done it all exchanged looks and began to murmur.

"She was right to leave me," Elliott said as his composure crumbled.

He pressed his thumb and forefinger into his eyes in an attempt to stave off more tears.

"I understand that now. She was right to save her life. I stand before you today seeking to save mine. I have the nice house and cars. I have the great job. I *had* a wife who loved me more than she loved herself, and I still couldn't get it right. I'm finally realizing that nothing but God can fill these deep, dark places in my soul where I hurt and feel inadequate. I'm asking you all to pray for God to help me."

Micah took the microphone from Elliott and turned to face him. He looked Elliott in the eyes and enunciated each word.

"Anybody can change, Elliott. All of us have access to God's grace.

"You and I have been at odds about this very issue for a long time. I stand here today promising to help you. We will pray for you here and hold you accountable, but it's your duty to seek anger management counseling. It's your responsibility to work at growing into the person God wants you to be."

Elliott nodded.

"I've tried for too long to do things my way," he said.

Micah called the worshipers forward for prayer, and everyone surrounded him and Elliott. Erika hesitated before rising from her seat. She reached for Charlotte's hand and Serena's. Because Aaron was sleeping, they stayed put in their row.

Erika bowed her head and joined in the group prayer for her broken husband.

Serena prayed too. Afterward, she raised her eyes to meet Erika's and realized they were thinking the same thing: If God could change a heart like Elliott's, nothing was impossible. Serena had known that about the Master for a long time, but today was deep reconfirmation.

When Micah ended the prayer, Donnie, a soft-spoken

ex-con who had served twenty years in prison for committing murder, sat at the keyboard and adjusted the microphone. The broad scar extending from his left earlobe to the center of his jaw seemed to deepen as he closed his eyes, threw back his head, and belted out Tonex's "Make Me Over."

Elliott turned to walk back to his seat. He looked up into the parting crowd and, for some reason, shifted his gaze to the left.

Serena saw him blink and blink again when he saw Erika, with her head still bowed in prayer.

42

Serena tugged at Erika's jacket. Erika opened her eyes, lifted her head, and found herself staring at Elliott, who looked as if he'd been doused with a bucket of cold water.

She wanted to bolt for the door but remembered that Charlotte and Serena were on either side of her. They would protect her. She sat down in her folding chair and tried to concentrate on the last few minutes of the service.

What if Elliott saw Aaron and tried to take him? What if he tried to force her to come with him?

She prayed silently as Micah spoke to the worshipers.

Lord, today is the day to face my past and walk toward my future. Is what I want right? Help me handle this.

By the time Micah had uttered, "Go in peace. Happy Easter!" Elliott had made his way to Erika's seat.

Charlotte stood and extended her hand, blocking Elliott's access to his wife.

"I'm Charlotte Gregory. I heard you up there and want you to know that I'm praying for you."

Elliott looked from Erika to Charlotte and back to Erika.

A scowl covered his face, but before he spoke it disappeared. He threw his hands up and shrugged.

"There's no need to protect Erika from me. I meant what I said up there a few minutes ago. I'm ready to change and put the past behind me."

Erika felt sucker punched. Was this for real?

She stared at Elliott without moving or speaking, until Aaron stirred in Serena's arms. Erika turned her head in their direction, and Aaron piped up, "Mommy!"

Elliott's eyebrows raised. He moved closer to Charlotte but looked past her, at the child in Serena's arms.

"I thought you and Micah had adopted a baby," he said. "Do you mean to tell me . . .?"

Erika took Aaron from Serena's arms and walked toward Elliott.

"Yes, we have a son, Elliott," Erika said. "His name is Aaron, and yesterday was his first birthday."

Elliott's mouth fell open.

Micah walked over and put his arms on Elliott's and Erika's shoulders.

"Why don't the four of us go into my office, so you can have some privacy?" Micah suggested, including Aaron in the group.

He led them to his study, closed the door behind them, and sat at his desk.

Erika thanked him with her eyes. She didn't want to be left alone with Elliott yet, regardless of what he had professed in church. She knew the worthlessness of empty promises. He could snap at any second and take off with her son.

Micah's actions indicated that he agreed.

The still-sleepy Aaron clung to Erika and laid his head on her shoulder, his eyes open just enough to take in the stranger who was his father. Elliott stood next to the chair Erika sat in and peered into his son's face.

"He's beautiful."

"Yes, he is," Erika said softly without looking at Elliott.

"May I sit next to you, Erika?"

She nodded but kept her eyes on Micah, who sat before her, watching silently.

"Can I talk to you?" Elliott pleaded.

Erika turned her gaze to him and rubbed her son's back.

"Go ahead."

Elliott took a deep breath.

"I meant what I said out there today. I saw Micah yesterday at the barbershop, and he said some things that made me take a long, hard look at myself. To be honest, they were things I've known for a long time. But when someone holds up a mirror and makes you confront your demons, you have to stop running from them at some point.

"I had decided that the failure of our marriage—starting with your disappearance—was all your fault and that you were wrong for leaving after all I had given you. I wasn't ready to confront my demons and my mistakes until Micah made me realize that you probably weren't coming back.

"Now today I find out that not only have I lost so much time with my wife, I've missed out on being a father. How could you have kept that from me?"

Erika's throat tightened as she struggled with the anger and other emotions she couldn't identify wrestling to erupt.

"How could I have told you, Elliott? Why would I want my son around a man who would teach him the wrong things about life, the wrong ways to treat a woman? How could I be sure you wouldn't have killed me to keep him all to yourself?"

Erika didn't utter the words with bitterness or malice, but they still caused Elliott to recoil as if he had been slapped.

She continued.

"For a long time, Elliott, I agreed with you. I thought I was doing something wrong, that I must deserve to be treated like scum and beaten like a dog. Why else would you be treating me that way? But when I walked away from our nightmarish life that night, I embraced reality; I finally embraced myself.

"I can't begin to tell you how hard it has been to spend the past year and a half living in a shelter with a dozen other women, or to have a baby and then give him away because I couldn't take care of him. But the things that don't break you make you stronger, Elliott.

"I've learned to love myself more than I ever have. I've learned that I can take care of myself. I know now that nobody has the right to treat me with anything other than respect and genuine love.

"I want the same for our son. Someday, after you get counseling and prove that you're capable of being a caring, responsible parent instead of an abusive one, maybe you can have a relationship with him. I'm not comfortable with that right now. I can't allow a batterer to have access to my son, not even if it's his father."

Pain blazed across Elliott's face.

"I deserve that. But what about the forgiveness and resurrection Micah talked about today?" Elliott pleaded. "Isn't there a chance for us to try again to be a family? I really want that, Erika."

Erika struggled to meet Elliott's eyes. She had once loved him so much that she thought she would die without him. When she realized she could breathe on her own, the fear of living without him dissipated. A part of her would always care for him, but she knew she could no longer be his wife.

She had prayed and prayed about how she could end her marriage and still please God. She still had no answers. But she knew God loved her unconditionally. He had proven himself faithful, even when she hadn't acknowledged his existence.

The more she had frequented Richmond to spend time with her son, the more Erika had accepted that an encounter with Elliott was going to be inevitable. She had wondered for the longest how she would handle this moment when it arrived. She had wondered how she would feel.

More than anything right now, she felt pity for the man who had been the love of her life, the anchor of her soul. His smothering, painful form of love had snuffed the life out of their marriage.

Erika, whose mother had floated from husband to boyfriend to husband, didn't want to put her child through the same existence.

As soon as she had voiced those fears to her dear friend Charlotte, Charlotte had dismissed them.

"You are not your mother," Charlotte had said. "People always talk about the positive influences making such a difference in children's lives. The negative ones can have just as much impact. They can teach you how *not* to be."

A mini movie flashed through Erika's mind as she reflected on the last two years of her life, marveling at how she had grown and the friends who had come to love and support her until she was strong enough to stand on her own. She thought about how moving into a shelter had helped her discover a gift and a love for interior design.

Serena had been so right when she said God knew how to turn the tartest lemons into the sweetest lemonade.

Erika looked at Elliott and shook her head. She couldn't change the way she felt, and she didn't really want to.

"I'm sorry, Elliott, but we can't go back. We've both grown and changed. For the better, I believe. We can't erase what happened between us or what has happened since we've been apart.

"I promise you this: you get the help you need to manage your anger, maybe even take a parenting class like I had to do at the shelter I lived in, and I'll let you have regular visits with Aaron. For my comfort level, they may be supervised at first, but we'll see from there."

"Is there someone else, Erika?"

She thought for a second before responding. She had grown to a place where she had no problem sharing the truth.

"I can honestly tell you no, Elliott. No one else has anything to do with the decision I've made to move forward with my life, to stand on my own and learn how to love myself by myself."

Aaron sat up on her lap and put his thumb in his mouth.

"You know better than that," Erika teasingly scolded him.

Elliott watched the boy and smiled.

"He looks mostly like you, but he has my smile and my nose. I can't believe I'm a father."

Elliott looked at Erika and then Micah, who had been watching the two intently while they talked.

"Can I hold him?"

Erika hesitated but assented when Micah nodded at her, reassuring her that he was on guard.

She passed Aaron to Elliott and watched as Elliott held the boy as if he were breakable and tried to talk to him.

"Hey, little man, what's your name?"

Aaron gurgled and smiled at him as he chewed on his thumb. Erika responded on his behalf.

"Aaron Tyler Wilson."

Elliott nodded.

"A fine name. I hope I'll get to know you well, Aaron Tyler Wilson. I'm going to do my best to be a better man so I can be a good father."

43

Melvin Gates, his wife, and his daughter, Kami, drove up just as Serena and Micah stepped out of the Audi. The Gateses had attended services at St. Mark's Baptist Church but were joining Serena and Micah for dinner.

Serena dashed up the short flight of stairs to open the front door for her guests.

"Come in and get comfortable," she told them as she trotted to the bedroom that had once been her mother's.

She paused and rested a shoulder against the doorway, looking at the king-size bed she and Micah had squeezed into the cozy room. Funny how life had a way of coming full circle.

Who would have thought she would have returned to the home she had fled when her mother had revealed the secret of her parentage? Who would have thought she would invite her biological father, his wife, and one of her half siblings for Easter dinner here?

Serena had sat in her car and wept on the day she and Micah had closed the sale of their Cobblestone Creek home to a couple with three children. Where would her own children be raised? Was she going to be blessed with any?

God had turned her thoughts that day to the biblical story of Hannah, who visited the temple daily to weep and pray for a child. He reminded her that Hannah went on to become the mother of Samuel, and because she was obedient and allowed Samuel to be raised in the temple by priests, she was blessed with other children—years after she had questioned whether she would ever conceive one child.

Serena had read those verses every day for the next month, thanking God in advance for her Hannah experience.

Despite Melvin's pleas for her to use the savings he had given her so she could keep the larger house and pay for in vitro, she had clung to God's promises that he would bless her and Micah for their faithfulness—spiritually, financially, and in their family life.

Slowly but surely, those prayers were being answered.

As word spread of New Hope Community Ministries' outreach into the city, area grocers began donating nonperishable foods and gift certificates for weekly food giveaways. Men, women, and teens who had never stepped foot inside a traditional church began to frequent the Saturday and Sunday services.

Some were still struggling with drug use, some needed better parenting skills, some came for the free food that was distributed after services, and some just wanted to hear a kind word.

When a young man named Bernard rose one night to share what had led him to the service, Serena locked eyes with Micah to make certain he knew that his reason for pouring their finances and his energy into this ministry had been worthwhile.

"I just left a street corner where a bullet whizzed by my ear," the jittery young man said in a booming voice. "I'm twenty-two years old, and I could have died tonight. I know who fired the shot. I know where I can find him. I had a gun in my pocket, and I could have pulled it out in a second."

The young man pointed at Micah.

"But I was here that night when he held up those sneakers. I knew that if I retaliated, the next pair of shoes Rev. Micah waved in the air could be mine.

"My boys looked at me like I was crazy when I told them I was coming here instead of going to find the shooter. They asked me if I'm going soft, if I'm lying down on them.

"I told them, naw—I ain't soft and I ain't scared. But if I'm going to be hard core, I want to do it for something that matters, like Rev. Micah said. Just because I escaped tonight don't mean it's over. But if I'm going to go out, I'm going out for God.

"I don't want to die on the street corner like my two brothers. My mama still cries for them every day. I want to be the one that lives, that makes her proud."

Tears and shouts of praise filled the school gym that night. Micah led them all in a long, heartfelt prayer, asking God to keep Bernard safe and to give him the courage to maintain his new perspective.

In the weeks that followed, Bernard's faith grew stronger. Micah and Serena weren't sure what he was telling his friends, but every so often young men who knew Bernard would stop by a service to see what had been able to so radically transform him.

Micah plainly told them that it wasn't him or the building or even the services. It was simple: Bernard's heart had been open to the seeds of God's goodness that Micah had planted there.

Serena was humbled by the realization that God was graciously allowing her and Micah to be part of the work he wanted done in the inner city. She knew that he was working everything else out too, in his own timing.

Erika was flourishing in her new career, and she still found time to drive down to Richmond and visit her son. It was heartwarming to see them together. Although she visited only twice a month, she and Aaron had developed a special bond.

Serena had been praying and preparing herself for the day when Erika would announce that she wanted to take Aaron home with her. She surmised it wouldn't be much longer, since Erika had recently moved out of the shelter.

Serena's heart ached at the thought of not having the sweet little boy to cuddle with, read to, or play silly games with. She would miss her morning routine of waking him by chewing on his cheeks.

God had granted her a temporary period of motherhood, and she wouldn't have traded it for the world. But she knew she would grieve when her house grew quiet upon his departure.

Serena entered the bedroom, which Micah had painted a muted gold, and pulled off her suit. Like Micah, she typically wore casual clothes to service but had spruced up for Easter today.

She grabbed her hair, twisted it into a chignon, and secured it with pins. After slipping into a pair of tan linen slacks with a matching semisheer top and slides, Serena felt ready to entertain.

She heard Charlotte's and Erika's laughter mingling with Melvin's and Tawana's. The clatter of little feet and jostling sounds told her Misha was chasing Aaron around his bedroom.

How she wished Mama were here today, in the flesh. She was the only one missing from this memorable gathering.

Serena dabbed at the single tear that fell from one of her eyes with her thumb and took a deep breath. Mama was here in spirit. She had to cling to that.

"Anybody hungry?" Serena asked as she emerged from her bedroom.

This Easter was already one for the record books. Who knew what would happen by the time she put the lamb on the table?

44

When everyone had changed into something more comfortable, they found seats around the modest dining room table.

Melvin asked Micah for the privilege of uttering the blessing.

"I thank God for family, no matter how we came to be. All of us here today are family, forever. May God bless this food and bless us all."

He leaned over and kissed his wife after uttering "Amen."

Althea echoed his sentiments.

"It's a blessing to be here, Serena and Micah. You two are my children just as Kami, James, and Perrin are. It's been a rocky road, but here we are, by God's grace.

"I would never try to take your mother Violet's place, but I'm here if you need me, Serena. We'll move forward as a family unit, no matter what."

Serena rose from her seat and hugged Althea.

Micah was reaching for the lamb, Charlotte for the yams,

and Ms. Carter for the rolls, when Tawana raised her hand and asked everyone to pause.

"Before we eat, can I share some news?"

After feigning annoyance, everyone sat back and looked at her expectantly.

Tawana laughed.

"Ya'll aren't that hungry. Micah didn't preach that long. Which, before I make my announcement, I want to comment on."

She turned toward Micah, who sat next to her, at the head of the table.

"I know you've been through a lot in the past year, with losing your job and trying to start a fledgling ministry. I want you to know that what I saw today blew me away. Never doubt that God has given you a powerful purpose. I'm proud to call you a friend and to have you as Misha's godfather."

Micah acknowledged her sentiments with an embarrassed smile and a nod.

"Enough about Micah," she said and waved him off to boisterous laughter. "Here's my news. Some of you around this table know I've dreamed of going to law school.

"Of course, my biggest obstacles have been how I would pay for it and how I would care for Misha while I'm in school. I found out yesterday that I've been accepted to Harvard Law as well as the law school at UVA."

Cheers interrupted.

"Both are offering free child care and scholarships."

Micah stood up and threw his napkin on his empty plate.

Serena walked around the table and joined him in enveloping Tawana in a hug that brought everyone, except Aaron and Misha, to tears.

"Can my mommy breathe in there?" Misha asked in a loud whisper.

The threesome ended their hug and wiped their eyes.

"I'm okay, baby," Tawana managed to mumble.

Serena took Tawana's hand and looked at Ms. Carter.

"This is proof of what God can do when we're faithful to him and true to ourselves. I'm so happy I can't think straight."

Serena hugged Tawana again and returned to her seat.

"Whoa," Micah said and smiled. He surveyed the table. "Anything else? If there's much more, we might as well skip dinner and just go straight to dessert."

Erika glanced at Charlotte and smiled.

"There is one little thing."

She saw Serena and Micah exchange looks.

"Yes, guys," she said solemnly. "The time is growing near to take the baby home with me. I have appreciated absolutely everything you have done for me and for Aaron. You've spent your own money, invested your hearts in him, and just treated him like he's your own.

"I want you to know that he is. Aaron will never be just another child to you. You are his parents as much as I am, and, I guess, Elliott will eventually be."

Erika moved forward.

"Here's what I want to share, though. D. Haven Interior Designs is letting me go from its northern Virginia store."

Serena frowned.

"Is this supposed to be good news?"

Erika smiled and nodded.

"Believe me, it is. My boss, Derrick, is planning to open a Richmond branch of the company. He has asked me to transfer to this location, since I'm a Richmond native. My connections and familiarity with the area will be helpful in growing the business.

"Derrick knew about my efforts to stay off Elliott's radar, so he hasn't been pushing. After all that happened today, though, I think I can hold my own living in the same city as Elliott. I'm going to tell Derrick I'll make the move."

Serena clapped her hands and smiled.

"You're moving here! We'll get to see you and Aaron regularly!"

Erika couldn't stop grinning. She looked like a kid loosed in a candy store.

"As soon as I can find a tenant to take over my half of the apartment rent, I'll move here. Derrick and Gabrielle will come down a couple times a week to oversee the office and will continue to help me prepare for the interior design licensing exam. I'll take some of my certification courses online, and Commonwealth University has a great interior design program I'm hoping to eventually enter."

Erika looked at her friends around the table.

"Keep me in your prayers. I'm starting over on my own, with a new career, soon to be caring for Aaron, and returning to the city I fled because of the abuse I suffered here.

"It was such a relief to clear the air with Elliott today. I can honestly say I'm praying for him. If God is willing, maybe we can all be friends."

Erika paused but raised her forefinger.

"I know everyone's hungry, but I just have to say one more thing. In all the time I've known Serena Jasper Mc-Daniels, she has been a beautiful person inside and out. Even when she called herself mad at God, there was still something about her that made her shine, that let me know she was different.

"Now I know that whether she knew it or not, God loved her too much to let her stray too far. Even when she didn't realize it, she had his favor.

"It took me a long time to appreciate the power and the value of a relationship with God. I had to do it the knuckle-head way—he brought me to my knees before I realized I needed him. But I'll tell you, I wouldn't change anything I've been through, because this journey has made me love God more deeply than I might have otherwise.

"I know it's not going to be easy raising Aaron on my own, but I know I have a lot of help. I also know it's not Oscar speech night, and the food is getting cold. Let's eat!"

Everyone laughed and applauded.

Micah looked into each face before reaching again for the platter of lamb.

"Misha? Aaron? Kami? Ms. Carter? Melvin? Althea? Charlotte? Serena? Any words?"

No one raised a hand, but Serena chuckled.

"This better be good," Micah said and sighed.

Serena laughed again.

"I'll be quick, since Erika took an hour."

Erika swatted at her friend.

"Erika, I just want to say that I've loved you like a sister for as long as I've known you. Micah and I have loved raising Aaron this past year.

"I've never told you that we had been trying every fertility treatment known to man when we got your call asking us to care for your baby. God orchestrated a way to meet both our needs at the right time.

"By allowing me to love Aaron, he has shown me that whether a baby comes from my womb or someone else's, I can still be the mother he has destined me to be. So thank you for that gift and for trusting me and Micah in that way."

Serena shifted her gaze to Micah, who sat at the other end of the table, opposite her.

"Micah, you've sacrificed so much to get New Hope Community Ministries off the ground. God is using you in such amazing ways. I'm just honored to be along for the ride."

Serena lowered her head for a second. Her voice was softer when she raised her eyes and continued. She was smiling.

"Because you're so busy with the ministry right now, I know you don't have much time to renovate or paint. But be thinking in the next few months about who can convert our garage into a nursery. The room Aaron is using is too small for twins."

Micah's eyes widened as her words sank in. Melvin clapped. Erika shook her head in amazement.

"*Twins?* Talk to me, Serena," Micah said just above a whisper.

"Happy Easter—Dad. I visited Dr. Ritter last week to talk about rescheduling the in vitro fertilization and told him I hadn't been feeling well. He sent me to Dr. Knott for a blood test, which confirmed that I'm seven weeks pregnant.

"Given my miscarriages and other problems, she did an ultrasound to make sure everything was okay. We both saw two heartbeats instead of one.

"Dr. Knott says everything looks great."

Serena rose and walked over to Micah, who had sat back in his chair and closed his eyes. He encircled her waist with his arms and laid his head on her belly, something he hadn't done for a long time. Serena beamed and rubbed his cheek.

"Our little bundles will be here in time for Christmas. I guess your gift won't be a surprise this year."

Acknowledgments

It would seem that writing a book is a solo project, one that begins and ends with the author. The truth is that throughout the process, people, places, incidents, circumstances, and most importantly, the heavenly Father, serve as muses. I thank God for making it so.

The way he orchestrates life so that even the words in a work of fiction can resonate with readers is a blessing. I thank him for allowing me to be one of his vessels.

I thank my husband, Donald, for being my first editor and for encouraging me in my writing endeavors. I thank my beloved children for being so supportive and for sharing me with my ever-present laptop (smile).

Gratitude is also due to my extended family, especially my siblings and my in-laws, for your love and continued support, and for being my biggest cheerleaders; to my writer friends Sharon Shahid and Teresa Coleman for reading portions of the manuscript and offering your candid insight; to my fellow authors Patricia Haley, Jacquelin

Thomas, Marilynn Griffith, Yolanda Young, Howard Owen, Laura Parker Castoro, Wayne Dawkins, and Tia McCollors for your advice and friendship; to Thurmond Alford Jr. for your insight into the interior design industry; to the Rev. Nathaniel D. West for helping with ministry details; to my agent Pamela Harty; to my editors at Revell Books; to my Trinity Baptist Church (Richmond) and Eighth Avenue Baptist Church (Arkansas) families; to the Midlothian chapter of Jack and Jill, Inc.; to my JSU family; and to my many, many encouragers.

Special thanks go to Muriel Miller Branch, Deborah Lowry, Kim Newlen, Angela P. Addison, Bobbie Walker Trussell, Margaret Williams, Joe and Gloria Murphy, Charmaine Spain, Hunter Henkel, Andy Taylor, Linda Dunham, Pam Perry, Gwendolyn Richard, Yolanda Butler, Elli Sparks, Scholar Cardwell, Karla Peters, Karen and Charlie Trotter, LaNessa West, Bonnie Newman Davis, Clarence and Michelle Oliver, Holly Alford, Ursula Murdaugh, Otesa Middleton Miles, Jeff and Tracy Street, Jeanie Southern, Rob and Cheryl Nelson, Mary Goodwyn, Sabrina Squire, Linda Pate, and Everett, Danita, Kristopher, and Kourtney Cannon.

To the readers, I pray that you have been entertained and blessed by the words in these pages. May God's unfailing love provide *just the right thing* to leave you thirsting no more.

In him,
Stacy

Stacy Hawkins Adams is an award-winning journalist and inspirational columnist. She also operates ClayWork Enterprises, a motivational speaking business. She and her husband, a minister, live in a suburb of Richmond with their two young children. She is also the author of *Speak to My Heart*. She welcomes readers to visit her website: www. stacyhawkinsadams.com.

Introducing **Marilynn Griffith** and the Shades of Style series

High fashion meets romance in the Big Apple for a fresh, funky designer. What will Raya do when she's charged with the task of designing a wedding dress for the woman who stole her fiancé?

ℜ **Revell**
www.revellbooks.com